W9-CFK-871

"Whoa, get this!" Louis exclaimed.

"This guy says he has a video of the ghost of Virginia Dare!" Louis began to read out loud: "Local resident Henry Crompton was making a video in the Elizabethan Gardens about nine o'clock in the morning. . . ."

He must have been the tourist I saw after I morphed, Alex thought.

"According to Crompton, 'I spotted a young girl with long hair darting through the bushes. At first I thought she was just another tourist, but then, before my eyes, she faded into the mist. Like a ghost. I knew it must be her—Virginia Dare.'"

"Hey, Alex," Louis said, laughing, "you were there yesterday morning. Did you see any ghosts wandering around?"

Alex noticed the worried look on Ray's face as he handed her the newspaper. There was a high-school photo of Henry Crompton, a harmless-looking teenager with a goofy grin on his face.

And next to that, another photo—a still from Henry Crompton's video.

Yikes! Alex thought. *That's not the ghost of Virginia Dare disappearing in the morning mist.*

It's a picture of me—in the middle of a morph!

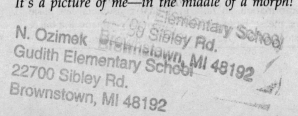
N. Ozimek
Gudith Elementary School
22700 Sibley Rd.
Brownstown, MI 48192

The Secret World of Alex Mack™

Available from MINSTREL Books

For orders other than by individual consumers, Pocket Books grants a discount on the purchase of **10 or more** copies of single titles for special markets or premium use. For further details, please write to the Vice-President of Special Markets, Pocket Books, 1633 Broadway, New York, NY 10019-6785, 8th Floor.

For information on how individual consumers can place orders, please write to Mail Order Department, Simon & Schuster Inc., 200 Old Tappan Road, Old Tappan, NJ 07675.

NICKELODEON®

the secret world of

ALEX MACK™

Sink or Swim!

Cathy East Dubowski and Mark Dubowski

A MINSTREL® BOOK

Published by POCKET BOOKS
New York   London   Toronto   Sydney   Tokyo   Singapore

The sale of this book without its cover is unauthorized. If you purchased this book without a cover, you should be aware that it was reported to the publisher as "unsold and destroyed." Neither the author nor the publisher has received payment for the sale of this "stripped book."

This book is a work of fiction. Names, characters, places and incidents are products of the author's imagination or are used fictitiously. Any resemblance to actual events or locales or persons, living or dead, is entirely coincidental.

A MINSTREL PAPERBACK *Original*

A Minstrel Book published by
POCKET BOOKS, a division of Simon & Schuster Inc.
1230 Avenue of the Americas, New York, NY 10020

Copyright © 1998 by Viacom International Inc., and RHI Entertainment, Inc. All rights reserved. Based on the Nickelodeon series entitled "The Secret World of Alex Mack."

All rights reserved, including the right to reproduce this book or portions thereof in any form whatsoever. For information address Pocket Books, 1230 Avenue of the Americas, New York, NY 10020

ISBN: 0-671-02108-7

First Minstrel Books printing July 1998

10 9 8 7 6 5 4 3 2 1

NICKELODEON, The Secret World of Alex Mack, and all related titles, logos and characters are trademarks of Viacom International Inc.

A MINSTREL BOOK and colophon are registered trademarks of Simon & Schuster Inc.

Cover photo by Pat Hill Studio

Printed in the U.S.A.

Sink or Swim!

CHAPTER 1

Alex Mack was bored.

Super bored.

Bored from the top of her purple crocheted hat to the tips of her bare toes sticking out of her sandals. And this was not just ordinary bored, the kind that could happen anywhere, any time of year, that could be fixed with a good book or an hour of playing video games or a phone call to a good friend.

This was bone-deep, gut-wrenching, middle-of-the-summer bored.

Of course, Alex loved summer vacation—*who didn't?* But after those first glorious weeks of summer there always came that day—somewhere between the Fourth of July and Labor Day—when you felt the same way you did after you'd gorged yourself on pizza and ice cream.

Without an appetite.

Alex felt like she'd stuffed herself on summer, and now she didn't have an appetite for doing anything.

She'd slept late. Read a ton of books. Hung out at the pool. Hung out at the mall. Enjoyed goofing off with no homework, project deadlines, or tests.

But doing nothing was fun only in contrast to doing too much. Without the contrast, it somehow lost its appeal.

Her parents had not been sympathetic at all.

Her father, George Mack, had repeated one of his favorite sayings: "Only boring people get bored, Alex." She hated it when grownups said that. And besides, her father was the kind of scientist who could spend hours all alone peering at a tiny speck under a microscope in his dreary lab at Paradise Valley Chemical Plant—and call it fun.

Her mother, Barbara Mack, was even worse. "If you're bored, Alex," she'd said pointedly, "I have a whole list of things that need to be done around the house. Starting with——"

Alex had suddenly "remembered" she had promised to meet her best friend Ray Alvarado and dashed out the door before her mother could put her to work scrubbing the grout between the tiles in the upstairs bathroom.

She'd rescued Ray from *his* father's cure for boredom—cleaning out the Alvarados' garage.

Together they'd escaped to the grassy slopes of Paradise Valley City Park, hoping that between the two of them they could come up with the perfect boredom buster. Now they lay back in the grass on a dandelion-covered hill, staring at a few puffy white clouds drifting across the bright blue sky.

"What do you want to do?" Alex asked Ray.

"I dunno. What do *you* want to do?"

"I asked you first."

"Yeah," Ray replied, "but I thought up yesterday's entertainment."

"Five hundred free throws?" Alex scoffed. "You call *that* entertainment?"

Ray shrugged. "It was the best I could do on

such short notice." He plucked a blade of grass and slowly began to tear it to shreds.

"Hey," Alex said. "We could . . ."

"Yes?" Ray asked hopefully.

Alex shook her head. "Nah . . ."

Ray's face fell, but then his eyes lit up. "How about—"

"What?" Alex asked with an eager smile.

"Never mind . . ." Ray flopped back onto the grass.

"This is terrible," Alex groaned. "It's enough to make you wish for school to start—"

"Al!" Ray shot back. "Bite your tongue!"

"Sorry."

The two fell silent, lying in the warm sun, so bored that not even the distant tinkle of the ice-cream man pushing his cart through the park could rouse them.

"Remember when we were kids, Ray?" Alex said with a sigh. They'd grown up together and been friends as long as she could remember. In fact, he was like the brother she had never had, only better, since they didn't fight like real siblings did and they solemnly kept each other's secrets.

Ray nodded and rolled onto his back, placing his hands under his head. "Those were the good old days. . . ."

"Summer *meant* something when we were little," Alex said. "I remember I couldn't wait to run out the door in the morning."

"Yeah, we never ran out of stuff to do back then."

Alex laughed. "Remember how our parents had to drag us into the house at night? We never wanted to go to bed. I used to get so many mosquito bites!"

"Me, too," Ray said with a laugh. "My dad always had to dunk me in the tub for an hour. Said the only way to wash a summer day off a kid was to *scrub* it off."

They laughed together, remembering the good times.

Then Alex frowned. "What did we used to do all day?"

"I don't know," Ray answered. "Played tag and stuff, I guess."

"Wanna play tag?"

"Not really."

"Me, neither." Alex sighed again, wistfully

this time. "I guess you can't go back and relive the past."

"I guess not," Ray agreed softly.

Together, they stared at the clouds some more. *It sure is tough being a teenager with nothing to do*, Alex thought. Idly she pointed her finger at a daisy growing twenty feet away and picked it telekinetically—with the powers of her mind— then began to pluck the petals from the flower one by one.

Ray started to warn her not to do that out in the open, where anybody could see, but he couldn't even rustle up enough energy for that. Besides, it was kind of neat to watch. "Hey, Al . . ."

Alex sighed. "Yeah, I know." She dropped her hand, and the delicate white petals drifted to the ground.

Alex had some unusual powers. On the first day of junior high school, she'd had a near-collision with a truck from Paradise Valley Chemical and had been doused by a barrel of a gold-colored, top secret, experimental chemical called GC-161. The driver of the truck had tried to chase her down, but she'd escaped to safety.

Only to discover, along with her genius older sister Annie, that her encounter with GC-161 had produced some very weird side effects.

Like she could zap things by shooting electrical charges from her fingertips. She could move objects with her mind—something her sister called telekinesis. And she could morph into what looked like a puddle. She could even grab hold of another person and morph him or her into the puddle, too.

But Annie had made her promise not to tell anyone. The head of Paradise Valley Chemical—Danielle Atron—would stop at nothing to find Alex and turn her into a human guinea pig for the plant. Annie and Ray were the only two people in the whole universe who knew her unusual secret.

"Want to morph or something?"

Ray shrugged. "Maybe later."

Having special powers was cool, but on a day like today, even being able to zap and morph couldn't save her from a case of the boredom blues.

Suddenly a shadow fell across them.

Alex and Ray shaded their eyes as they looked up into the face of a kid in dark glasses.

" 'Sup, guys?" Louis Driscoll raised his sunglasses to stare down at them over his freckled nose. "You look like you've been run over by the ice-cream man."

"Thanks a lot, Louis. We're just bored out of our minds."

"Well, then," Louis said smugly, "you *are* glad to see me."

"Sure, Louis," Alex said without enthusiasm.

But Louis just grinned like a little kid who was about to spill a secret. A big secret. "I," he announced proudly, "am here to save you from your boring lives."

Alex and Ray didn't get excited. In fact, they didn't even move. They were used to Louis's schemes, plans, and "awesome" ideas. Usually they involved big dreams and a request to borrow cash—and just as often resulted in somebody getting into hot water.

"What is it this time, Louis?" Ray asked without opening his eyes.

"Did I ever mention my uncle Stephen and aunt Laura?" Louis asked as he sat down on the grass beside them.

"Maybe . . ." Ray replied with a yawn.

"He's my dad's younger brother," Louis explained. "Corporate attorney for a major company. Aunt Laura was some kind of business executive or something, I think. They're really cool."

"That's nice, Louis," Alex said automatically.

"But wait, here's what I need to tell you guys," Louis went on. "They live in Chicago. I mean—make that past tense. Lived."

Alex shifted up onto one elbow and gazed at Louis sympathetically. "I'm sorry, Louis."

"But why?"

"What happened?" Ray asked gently. "Car accident?"

Louis rubbed a frustrated hand through his curly reddish-brown hair. "No, no, no. They *weren't* in an *accident!* They don't live in Chicago anymore because they *moved!*"

"Oh," Alex said, then frowned in confusion. "But how's that going to save us?"

"I'm trying to tell you," Louis said impatiently. "They dropped out of the rat race in the big city. Chucked the whole yuppie thing. And get this—my uncle bought an actual *dive* shop on the Outer Banks of North Carolina. Scuba diving—isn't that cool?''

"We're happy for him," Ray mumbled. "Send him our regards."

Louis rolled his eyes. "I'm not finished yet, Ray. Do you mind? They've invited me to come visit them for a week—"

Alex opened one eye. "Oh, hey, lucky you."

"—*and* bring along a *couple of friends* if I want to!" Louis's brown eyes gleamed as he paused, letting the news sink in.

"And I am currently taking nominations," he added.

Alex and Ray sat up suddenly.

"You mean, like, we can go with you?" Alex exclaimed, brushing her blond hair off her cheek. "On a trip?"

"This is like the Atlantic Ocean, right?" Ray asked. "What'd you call it? The Outer Beltway?"

"The Outer *Banks*," Louis corrected him. "It's a string of barrier islands off the coast of North Carolina where Blackbeard hid his pirate ships. And, you know—where the Wright Brothers made the first manned airplane flight. I've never been there, but my cousin Megan wrote me and says it's really terrific. She says the beaches there are the best. You'd like her, Alex. She's a year older than us and she's pretty cool. For a cousin, that is."

"So when are you going?" Alex asked excitedly. "And are we *really* invited—for *real?*"

"Sure," Louis replied. "My mom and dad can't get out there right now, because of work, and my aunt and uncle thought it would be more fun for me if I brought some friends." His freckled face broke into a grin. "So do I take it you're interested? I promise—you won't be bored out there."

"Are you kidding?" Alex exclaimed, jumping to her feet. "Come on—let's go ask my mom and dad!"

"Outer *where?*" Alex's dad wanted to know. Alex explained, and after her dad thought about it, he took decisive action. "Go ask your mother," he answered.

Mrs. Mack had another idea. "Go ask your father," she suggested.

Eventually everybody got together and after a few phone calls between Alex's family, Ray's family, and Louis's family—in Paradise Valley and across the country in North Carolina—the trip was on.

Then it took a lot of planning and packing and lectures on safety until they were finally ready to go.

"I just have one final question," Mr. Mack said at last. Turning to Mrs. Mack, Alex's dad said, "Outer *where?*"

CHAPTER 2

It took three planes to get them to Norfolk, Virginia, and they were still a long car ride from their destination.

Louis's uncle Stephen was waiting for them at the gate. He was tall with longish dark hair and an easygoing smile, dressed in a loose-fitting black hooded sweatshirt, jeans, and white athletic shoes. The sweatshirt was decorated with a little dive flag over the heart and a line underneath that read "Graveyard Divers," the name of his shop.

"Hi, guys," he said. He looked genuinely pleased to see them all. Then he reached out a hand to Louis. "What's happening, Louis?"

"Hi, Unc," Louis said.

They shook hands formally, and then suddenly Stephen said, "Ah, what the hey," and grabbed his nephew in a big bear hug. "Good to see you, pal."

"Alex, Ray—this is my uncle—Mr. Stephen Driscoll."

"Call me Stephen," Louis's uncle said to them.

"Uncle Stephen, meet Alex Mack and Ray Alvarado."

"Alex," Alex said, shaking hands.

"Ray."

"Let's get your bags," Stephen said. "Laura and Megan can't wait to see you."

"So how come Megan didn't come with you, Uncle Stephen?" Louis asked as they all walked to the baggage claims area. "She still mad at me for creaming her at tennis last summer?"

Stephen laughed. "Better watch out, Hot Shot. She's been taking lessons, and she's got a killer backhand she's just dying to try out on you!"

"This I gotta see!" Louis said.

"Megan wanted to come," Stephen explained as they stopped at the baggage carousel in the lower level of the airport. "But she had to work."

"Work?" Louis exclaimed. "Megan? You've got to be kidding. I thought she was allergic to work."

"It's amazing what a paycheck will do," her dad joked.

Alex spotted her bag, and walked up to grab it. "What kind of job did she get?" she asked Stephen.

"She's working at a shop on the beach called Tropical Tees," Stephen said. "Airbrushing T-shirts."

"Wow," Alex said. "That sounds cool. Is she an artist?"

Stephen nodded. "She's pretty good, too. The owner has even begun to let her do some of her own designs."

Louis snagged his bag. "This I gotta see."

Stephen shook his head and confided in Alex and Ray, "You guys better watch out for them. They've got this sibling rivalry thing going— even though they're only cousins."

"What's an only child supposed to do?" Louis protested. "I gotta pick on somebody."

It was a two-hour drive from the airport to the beach town called Nags Head where the Driscolls lived. On the way down, the view outside Stephen's truck changed from city streets to swampland to farm fields to the spectacular view of a wide expanse of water spanned by a long bridge that zigzagged over the water all the way to the horizon.

They took the bridge to the other side of the water and a town called Manteo on an island named Roanoke—Indian words, Stephen explained. Then they took another shorter bridge from that island to one farther east with sand dunes, stores, hotels, cottages, and condominiums along a single, wide road.

The signs along the road all indicated Alex and Ray were a long way from Paradise Valley. Restaurants like Dune Burger, the Wharf, and Tale of the Whale. Condominiums with yacht parking. Sporting goods stores called Wave Riding Vehicles, Whalebone, and Vitamin Sea. A hang-gliding school. And hotels named after the water that seemed to be on everyone's mind: Sea Foam, Sea Spray, Ocean Side.

The brisk breeze smelled fresh and clean and salty.

"I can get into this," Louis told Ray. "We've

been living in the desert too long. I'm ready to catch some waves."

"But this is kind of a desert, too," Alex said. The side of the road was bright with sand lit by the setting sun. Where the drifts had a chance to catch the wind and build up into dunes, it looked like a picture of the Sahara Desert.

Stephen pulled off the road at a billboard sign for Jockey's Ridge, a city park–size mountain range of sand dunes packed into the middle of the town. They all got out and climbed the path to a peak that gave them a seagull's-eye view of the town—and of the water that stretched away in both directions. To the east, the waves of the Atlantic Ocean sparkled under the stars. In the other direction, the smooth flat sound stretched to Manteo.

"What a view!" Ray exclaimed. But just then the wind kicked up, sweeping a stinging cloud of sand over the peaks and driving them all back down to the Jeep.

At a place called Captain Bill's, Stephen slowed the truck and turned right, taking the driveway up to and underneath a two-story cottage where he stopped next to a wooden stair-case. The sky was dark and there were no streetlights, but the parking area underneath the house was cheerful in the light of bare electric bulbs spaced along the beams. "The ocean's right across the street," Stephen told them as they emptied the Jeep. From the top of the driveway they could see the breakers trailing white along the beach in the moonlight.

A woman and a teenage girl hurried down the stairs to meet them.

"If this place isn't the end of the road, I don't know what is!" Laura said. *It really is*, Alex thought. *If you wanted to go any farther you'd need a boat.*

The woman—clearly Aunt Laura—threw her arms around Louis and hugged him till he blushed. "Louis, I can't believe how much you've grown!" she exclaimed. When she finally let go, he turned to his cousin.

"Hey, creep," he said affectionately. "I hear you lost your mind and got a job."

Megan punched her cousin in the arm. "I didn't lose it—I found it," she retorted with a grin. "So don't even *think* of hitting me up for a loan, little cousin."

"Little?" Louis exclaimed, glaring up into the face of his cousin, who stood a good four inches taller than he did. "You're barely eight months older than me," he reminded her. "That barely counts."

Stephen rolled his eyes and told Alex and Ray in a stage whisper, "What'd I tell you about these two? They're crazy about each other!"

"*Ewwwwwww!*" Louis and Megan said at the same time.

Alex grinned. It was obvious, despite their verbal sparring, that Louis and Megan were pretty close.

But then Megan pushed past her cousin and grabbed Alex by the arm. "I'm *so* glad you're here, Alex. I've heard so much about you. And I don't know what I'd have done if I was stuck here all week with just Louis to pester me!"

Alex laughed. "Well, I'm glad to be able to rescue you!"

Megan was tall and slim and already tan, and she wore an oversize T-shirt with an airbrushed painting of a dolphin leaping out of the water.

"Is this one of your designs?" Alex asked.

Megan nodded.

"I love it!" Alex said truthfully.

"Thanks!" Megan replied, obviously pleased. "The job is so cool! I have a few days off, since you guys are here, but I want to take you to the shop. My boss, Candy, is so nice."

"I hear her son is pretty nice, too," Stephen said with a twinkle in his eye.

"Dad!" Megan exclaimed as a faint blush stole across her cheeks. Then she whispered to Alex, "His name's Henry, and he's sort of my boy-friend—but don't tell Louis!"

"Promise!" Alex whispered back, and they giggled together like old friends.

Megan's bright friendly smile and easy chatter made Alex like her right away, and she was glad they were sharing Megan's room.

Then the Driscolls led them up the wooden steps to the extensive deck that wrapped around the cottage's first floor. Alex loved it at once. It was spacious and homey—the kind of place where you could relax and not worry about ruining the furniture. But there was something very odd about it.

"Why's your house upside down?" Louis blurted out.

Alex elbowed him in the ribs. "Louis!" Tact was not one of Louis's strong points. But he had a point. All the bedrooms were on the first floor. Which meant the living area and kitchen were upstairs.

But Laura just laughed. "You'll see."

Alex dropped her bags off in Megan's room—Ray and Louis were sharing the guest room at the end of the hall. Then they followed the Driscolls upstairs to the top floor.

Alex stopped in the middle of the room and stared. "Wow . . ." she said.

"That's exactly what I said the first time I came up here!" Laura said with a laugh.

The room had two sets of sliding glass doors that opened out onto another wraparound deck; huge windows filled the other walls. Looking out one side of the house Alex could see the moon reflecting on the ocean. Out the other side she could see across the lights of houses to the sound and in the distance the lights of Manteo.

Megan came up beside her. "We get the sunrise over the beach on this side, and the sunset over the sound on that side." She sighed. "It's the most beautiful place I've ever been. Wait till you see the sunrise. You won't believe it."

Louis let out a low whistle. "This place must have set you back a bundle, Uncle Stephen."

Megan groaned. "Only you would look at something like this and think of real estate values, Louis."

Louis shrugged. "What'd I say?"

Stephen led them out onto the deck, where a brisk breeze rustled Alex's hair. The hushed roar of the waves endlessly pounding the beach was hypnotic and soothing.

"It's not about real estate," Stephen told his nephew. "Our home back in Chicago was bigger than this—fancier, too." He slipped an arm around Laura's shoulders. "I spent the last twenty years of my life holed up in high-rise office buildings, working under fluorescent lights, surrounded by concrete, with the only scraps of nature stuck behind the fences of city parks. But look around you—here we're living right in the middle of nature." He shook his head. "Louis, I've never felt more alive."

Louis nodded. "I guess I'm beginning to see why you guys dropped out of the rat race."

"We didn't drop out, Louis," Laura said. "We chose something better."

Alex and Ray exchanged a smile. They had really lucked out to have a chance to visit here. Great hosts, a great beach—it was going to be an awesome week!

They all sat out on the deck for a bit, talking and getting to know one another, but it was late, so soon Megan led Alex down to her room. Megan's bed had a trundle that pulled out from underneath to make another single for Alex, and she'd cleared out a drawer in her dresser for Alex, too.

"I hope you like it here," Megan said. "I certainly do. There's something special about living here—a block from the ocean instead of a block from the health club."

"Weren't you sad to leave your friends back in Chicago?" Alex asked as she began to change into her nightgown.

Megan shrugged. "Yeah, that was the hard part. At first I didn't want to come. All I'd ever known was living in the city. But the people who live here year round are really nice, and I've made new friends pretty easily. And every night I go to sleep to the sound of the waves. Every morning I go for a walk on the beach. I really love it—except for that nor'easter when we first moved down here—"

"What's that?" Alex asked.

"When a big storm blows in off the ocean out of the northeast, they call it a nor'easter. The wind and rain can last anywhere from a couple of days to a couple of weeks. This one lasted even a little longer. It seemed like the wind would never quit, and when I lay on the floor—it was awesome. I could hear the wind flowing over and under the house. When we got a big long gust, the whole house kind of trembled on the pilings, like we were going to take off through the air. It was amazing. After the storm I went out on the beach and found these—" She pointed to two dark gray conch shells on her dresser. They were perfectly shaped and undamaged by their journey in from deep water offshore.

"That's not the only kind of thing you can find out here," Megan continued. "There are hundreds of shipwrecks on the bottom of the ocean around here—pirate ships, fishing boats, German submarines—you name it. Storms that bring in seashells can bring in stuff from the wrecks, too. People have found all kinds of artifacts right on the beach—even whole boats have come in."

Alex found that almost impossible to imagine.

"There's part of one boat that's buried under the beach not too far from here," Megan said. "In the wintertime, when the beach erodes, it shows up on the beach, like it just landed. You never know what the ocean's going to bring you."

Later, lying in bed by the open window in Megan's room, Alex listened to the distant rumble of the surf and wondered what it had in store for her.

At six the next morning Megan's room was full of sunlight—because there was nothing between the house and the eastern horizon except wide open ocean, mornings started bright and early at the Driscolls'.

Alex, Ray, Louis, Megan, and Laura were all upstairs in the kitchen with pancakes on the table before the sun was much more than a big red ball bobbing on the horizon.

"I'm taking you guys back over the bridge to Manteo this morning," Megan told them. "There's an old fort, an outdoor theater, and these huge Elizabethan Gardens—we'll take the Jeep so I can also show you around the area. Then after lunch we'll catch up with Dad—he had to get some divers ready at the shop this morning."

Riding in the open Jeep, the salt air was refreshing and cool. Alex rode in front with Megan, and Ray and Louis shared the bench seat in back.

"There were a lot more cars out last night," Alex noticed. The streets seemed almost deserted now.

"Half the houses around here are summer vacation cottages, rented out by the week," Megan explained. "So there's not a lot of people going to work—the early risers mostly walk down to the beach. Plus the stores don't open until ten. My dad's shop is different—divers want an early start because it takes an hour or two for the boat to get them out to where they want to go."

They pulled into a small parking area and followed a half-buried wooden boardwalk between two dunes onto the beach.

Soft white sand turned darker and harder as they went down to the water. At the high water mark the tide had left a ribbon of shell fragments down the beach as far as they could see. Every fifty yards or so someone was peering into it, looking for hidden treasures.

Below the shells the sand was dark gray and smooth as pavement—except, Alex noticed, where there was a double line of tire tracks.

"Beach patrol," Megan explained. "In the summer only the patrol and local net fishermen are allowed to drive on the beach. In the wintertime anybody with four-wheel drive can. Over on the national park beaches you can drive year round."

"Nice way to check out the waves," Ray said.

"Yeah, as long as you don't get stuck," Megan said. "And get caught by the tide."

"Ouch," Louis said.

After a few minutes on the beach, they headed back to the Jeep and took the road past Captain

Bill's Hot Dog House onto the main highway heading for the bridge over the sound.

When they were on Roanoke, the island between the Atlantic Ocean beaches and the mainland, the "desert look" of the ocean islands changed to forest. They followed the main road through the sleepy-looking town of Manteo to a waterfront park that was the site of an old English fort some four hundred years ago. The fort was gone, but paths through the woods showed the positions of the ramparts and cannons that defended the island against Spaniards and others also interested in setting up housekeeping in the New World.

Ray and Louis decided to explore the fort while Alex and Megan went through the Elizabethan Gardens next door.

"We'll catch up with you guys at the gates to the Elizabethan Gardens in about a half-hour," Megan said.

Beyond the gate, the gardens were a world unto themselves, seemingly unconnected to the life on the outside. Sand and cobblestone paths wound through formal gardens that seemed as if they had been transported there from another time. The morning air still held a light mist that gave everything a beautiful, surreal kind of feeling.

Alex strolled through gardens of herbs, roses, and native and exotic plants, losing herself in the mood of the place—and losing herself from Megan in the process.

She didn't notice they'd gotten separated until the sight of another young woman in the mist surprised her—a ghostly figure in the clearing.

Alex felt drawn to her.

When she got closer, she could see it was a statue of a young woman named Virginia Dare, the first English child born here in the New World in 1587. How she looked was from the artist's imagination—the real girl had been only a baby when she and the whole town of settlers vanished without a trace in 1590. It was still an unsolved mystery, and they were known as the "Lost Colony."

As Alex admired the statue, she wondered what might have happened to young Virginia Dare. Were the colonists attacked? Had they left for another place?

Suddenly she heard voices.

Voices of two men in the mist. They were approaching her on the path, unaware of her presence. Something in the tone of their voices made Alex duck behind a hedge.

One was young and the other was old.

The younger man was blond and good-looking, with a dark tan, dressed in shorts and a colorful casual shirt. He was showing the older man some kind of small objects that she couldn't see.

"Here's a good place," she heard the young blond man say. "There's nobody around. See? I told you this would be better than talking at your hotel. We can talk in complete privacy."

The older man humphed. "Fine, then. Let's get down to business. My time—my client's time— is valuable. Show me the goods."

Alex ducked. She didn't know why the men didn't want anyone around—but they might get mad if they saw her.

The younger man stopped in the path and opened a small duffel bag on the ground. Then he removed something—Alex couldn't tell what—and handed it to the older man.

It looked like a piece of something. Made of metal.

The older man turned the object over in his hand and said something Alex couldn't hear, then replied, in a deep voice tinged with some kind of foreign accent, "Mr. K would be interested in this—and other objects—from the same location."

"I knew he'd be interested," the younger man said. "I just need to know how much."

"How much are you asking?" the other man replied.

"Well, I'm not sure. This particular location is not as easy to get to as some of the others. It's somewhat risky, if you know what I mean—legally."

The man with the accent gave back the object, took out a wallet, and counted out several bills. The younger man smiled, took the money, and handed over the duffel bag.

"There will be more?" the older man asked.

The young man chuckled. "That's just the warm-up," he answered, pushing the cash into a nylon billfold.

Whatever they were doing was secret *and* worth a lot of money. What could it be?

Alex had stayed frozen in a crouch for as long as she could bear. She tried to shift her weight and suddenly felt herself starting to fall over backward—

"Whoops."

Startled, the two men looked around.

"Who's there?" the blond man called out.

Alex felt her face go stone cold. She was about to be caught eavesdropping.

Listening in on something that clearly neither she nor anyone else was supposed to have heard.

CHAPTER 3

Without thinking, Alex did what any normal girl would do.

Any normal girl with not-so-normal powers.

She morphed.

Thinking of water usually helped her morph, and here, with the Roanoke Sound just yards away, it was easy.

Alex felt that familiar tingle throughout every atom of her body, and then—*ka-WHOOSH!* It was like swooshing down a waterslide and then melting into a puddle. With a gurgle, she scooted off along the sandy paths, hoping the men wouldn't notice a mobile spill as they searched the bushes for their eavesdropper.

Careening around a hedge, Alex sloshed to a halt when she spotted legs up ahead. Her vision was a tiny bit distorted when in her morphed form—sort of like looking up from the bottom of a swimming pool. But the person in the path didn't seem to be either of the men she'd over-heard. *Just a tourist*, she realized as she noticed his shorts and sandals. He appeared to be mak-ing a home video of the gardens.

Steadying her nerves, she detoured around him and headed for the gate. Behind a bush, she re-formed.

Despite the fact that the sun was over the tree-tops now and warming up for another hot one at the beach, Alex was shivering a little as she caught sight of Megan, Ray, and Louis at the gate.

"Hi, guys," she said. Her voice sounded nervous.

"Did you get lost?" Megan asked. "I'm sorry we got separated. I just turned around and you were—"

"I know," Alex said. "Gone. Poof! I have a habit of doing that sometimes."

"I was telling Megan you guys should have gone with us to the fort," Ray said. "Maybe we could have found some old artifacts around there." He gave Alex a knowing look.

Ray knew Alex could morph and move objects with the power of her thoughts.

But a metal detector she was not.

"Sorry, Ray." Megan smiled. "State archaeologists have gone over that site with a fine-toothed comb. Plus it's kind of a rule that anything you do find around here that might have historical importance should be turned over to the state. Depending on where you find it, you can even be legally required to give up your 'treasure.' "

"Whatever happened to 'Finders keepers, losers weepers'?" Ray wanted to know.

"A lot of people say that," Megan replied. "It comes up a lot at my dad's dive shop. When a diver finds something interesting that's fifty or a hundred years old on an old shipwreck, who does it belong to?"

"I think the diver gets to keep it," Ray said.

"He went to the trouble of going down and getting it."

Megan started toward the Jeep. "What if it's something personal—something that belonged to a victim? Maybe it should be returned to the family of the person who it originally belonged to."

"What if it was some kind of cargo with a lot of value," Louis said. "Say it was insured—maybe the insurance company would have a claim to it."

"Or the government," Megan said. "If it has some historical value, the state claims it on behalf of its citizens, and it winds up in a museum. Unless some collector gets to it first. My dad'll tell you that an unethical diver can make pretty good money if he or she finds the right wreck—and the right collector."

"Then the artifact is like hot merchandise?" Ray asked.

"Hey, speaking of hot," Louis said, "has anyone else noticed that the temperature has gone up about a hundred degrees since this morning?"

It was only eleven o'clock but the thermometer was already in the eighties.

Megan suggested they hit the beach before lunch.

Back at the house, everyone changed into swimsuits, Alex putting on a new electric blue one-piece she'd bought just for this trip.

The Driscolls' house was right across the street from a wooden-plank walk that led through a patch of sea oats between two cottages and around a dune down to the beach. On the way out, Megan grabbed two foam boards from the ground-level storage closet built behind the staircase. A minute later they were there.

The beach that had been empty this morning was now packed with families and teenagers enjoying the beautiful day. Colorful triangular kites that Megan called "delta wings" danced on the strong ocean breeze, and dozens of vacationers bobbed in the rollers just beyond the shore break.

"So who shrunk your surfboard?" Louis asked his cousin.

Megan dropped the foam boards on the sand and laughed. "You're a nut, did you know that, Louis? These are boogie boards. They're for body surfing."

Louis put on his I-knew-that face. He used it when he *didn't*.

"Come on, I'll show you," Megan said.

She led Louis through the wash at the edge of the water and out to the white rows of breaking waves. They hopped through them sideways, to keep from getting knocked over, until they were in the smoother water on the other side.

Holding the front edge of her board with both hands, Megan lay down on it and waited for a swell to come in and lift her like a cork. When it did, she kicked hard to get ahead of the peaking crest and slipped into the curl. As the wave broke behind her, it pushed the lightweight board toward the sand, giving her a fast ride to the beach.

Her cousin was next. Dragging Louis, the board didn't move quite as quickly as it had in front of Megan, but Louis still got a pretty good ride the first time.

Ray and Alex sat down on two of the Driscolls' yellow-striped beach towels while Louis and Megan went out again.

Ray slipped his wraparound sunglasses on and stretched out in the sun. "Now, this is the way to spend summer," he said with a sigh.

Alex laughed. She couldn't help but notice that Ray was stretched out just the way he was that day they were bored out of their minds. *What is so different?* she wondered. They were still goofing off, but with the ocean breeze and the sound of the surf, she seemed more awake— more alive.

Alex shaded her eyes with her hand and searched the waves for Louis and Megan.

And gasped.

A chill went down her back as she spotted a blond-headed guy coming toward them on the high part of the beach. Wasn't he the one she'd seen in the gardens that morning?

But then he turned his eyes to the water, and Alex saw his profile and relaxed. Not the same guy at all. It was only a teenage lifeguard, surveying the waves.

"Hey, Al," Ray asked, squinting up at her. "What's wrong?"

"Nothing," she said at first. Half of her wanted to tell Ray what she'd heard that morning in the gardens and the other half wanted to forget all about it.

The half that wanted to tell won. "I just thought I saw somebody. Somebody I saw in the gardens this morning."

Ray shrugged. "Probably a tourist."

"No, Ray." Alex dug her toes into the warm sand and wrapped her arms around her knees. "I heard these two men talking in there—after I got separated from Megan. They thought they were alone." She told him what she'd heard. "Do you think I should tell somebody?"

Ray frowned. "Tell who?"

"I don't know." Alex picked up a long shell and began to dig in the sand. "The police or somebody."

"The *police?*" Ray sat up and looked at her. "You gotta be kidding, Alex. Tell them what?"

Alex shrugged. She wasn't sure. "Whatever they were doing, they were hiding. And whatever they were hiding, they were going to do again. The blond guy said it was just the warm-up."

"Hey, Al—we're on vacation, remember? We're supposed to be having the time of our lives! Who cares what a couple of weird dudes were whispering about in the gardens?" He jumped to his feet and yanked Alex up by the hand, dragging her toward the water. "Come on! It's our turn to do the boards!"

Alex allowed herself to be pulled toward the ocean, letting the sound of the breakers wash the men's strange conversation from her mind.

It didn't take too much time on the boards before they were all starving.

"To Captain Bill's!" Megan cried.

"To Captain Bill's! To Captain Bill's!" the others shouted.

They grabbed the boards, wrapped their personal things in the towels, and made a mad dash for the house. There everything got thrown in the back of the Jeep and they all hopped in for the ride over to Captain Bill's Hot Dog House.

There was a short line of customers waiting on the wooden steps in front of the restaurant.

After the swim and the breezy ride in the Jeep, the wait in the sun outside the restaurant made the heat especially noticeable.

"I'll bet it hits a hundred degrees by this afternoon," Louis said.

"I'll bet I hit the water again this afternoon, too," Alex said.

Megan smiled. "I'll bet you do, too," she said with a secretive smile.

A few minutes later they were inside.

Captain Bill's served only lunch in a clean, white-painted plywood-paneled room consisting of dinette tables with a central counter where you placed and picked up your order.

The menu: hot dogs. Nothing but hot dogs.

Anything but boring, though!

Captain Bill, who was there live and in person seven days a week, had discovered fifty-two ways to serve hot dogs—fifty-two and counting.

The Captain's motto was proudly displayed at the top of the menu board bearing the fifty-two choices: WRECK A HOT DOG WITH THE CAP-

TAIN. Each hot dog on the menu was named after a local shipwreck.

No problem, Alex thought. They had come prepared to do serious wreckage.

"I'll have a *U-85*," Louis told the Captain. The U-85 was named after a German submarine, and came with sauerkraut. Ray tried a Tug, a hot dog with "spare-tire fenders" made of sliced black olives, and Megan had a *Lizzie S. Haynes*, a hot dog with three pretzel sticks named after a three-masted schooner that sank in 1889.

Alex picked the *Queen Anne's Revenge*, named after the flagship of the famous pirate Blackbeard. It came with a tiny skull-and-crossbones flag on a toothpick flagpole stuck into the hot dog bun.

Alex rolled the toothpick between her thumb and forefinger, fanning the little pirate flag. "Wouldn't it be cool to discover a famous shipwreck?" she said.

"Hey, you're in the right place for it," Louis said. "They don't call the waters around these islands the 'graveyard' for nothing, you know."

"Yeah, right," Alex said. "If you're a scuba diver—which you can't even do until you're eighteen."

"Uh-uhn!" Ray objected. "You don't have to scuba dive to find wrecks around here—right, Megan?"

Megan smiled. It was time to let the cat out of the bag. She handed Alex a folded sheet of paper from her back pocket. "It's kind of like a treasure map," she said. "Dad's taking us wreck hunting this afternoon!"

Alex unfolded the paper. It was Graveyard Divers stationery. At the top of the page was a drawing of a hot dog bun marked "Bill's" to stand for the restaurant. A dotted line connected it to a simple drawing of a ship with stick masts marked *Laura A. Barnes.*

The dotted line gave the heading and distance: South on Highway 24, 37 miles.

"Aunt Laura packed four sets of snorkeling gear in the Jeep for us," Megan told them. "Dad'll meet us at the wreck."

"Don't we need a boat or something?" Alex asked.

Megan smiled. "You'll see."

*   *   *

Ten minutes after they left the parking lot everything had changed. The shops, hotels, and cottages disappeared. The view on both sides of the highway turned into a desert landscape of sand dunes and short, muscular-looking trees with upper branches that grew in shapes determined by the wind.

It stayed that way for miles. The sand dunes on their left formed a kind of wall that held back the sea. Now and then they came to a place where the sea had broken down the wall. Here they could see a beach and the ocean stretching to the horizon.

"Look at all the sandbags," Megan said. The park service was rebuilding a dune that the water and wind had eroded away. Allowed to run its course, the break in the dunes would spread and blowing sand would eventually cover the highway.

On the other side of the highway, off to the right, the big difference was the plant life that had taken hold.

Desert scrub, mainly, hiding a creek that flashed its presence in the sun here and there. Beyond the scrub in the distance they saw a line of trees, and beyond the trees they saw another body of water spreading across the western horizon—the Pamlico Sound. The sound was cradled between the mainland and the sand barrier islands. They were on a hundred-mile ribbon of sand that was the Cape Hatteras National Seashore.

Alex kept an eye on the odometer as it counted up the miles to the *Laura A. Barnes.* "We're almost there," she told Ray. Right on time they saw a sign—Coquina Beach—and pulled into a sand-swept concrete parking area.

Megan pulled up beside a white powerboat on a trailer behind a familiar-looking pickup truck. It was Stephen—he looked up from the stern of the trailered boat—holding a pair of floatation vests. He grinned and tossed the vests to the front of the boat.

"Hey, I see you guys found it," he said. "Your first wreck, huh? She's over there." He pointed at a break in the dunes, a natural-looking passage.

The wreck of the *Laura A. Barnes* lay half-buried in the sand.

"It looks like a big rib cage," Alex said. The

timbers were blackened and worn from the weather.

"She was on her way from New York to South Carolina when a storm caught her," Stephen said. He'd followed them from the parking area. "Blew her right up on the beach. That was the good thing about it—nobody drowned."

"What kind of ship was she?" Alex wanted to know. It was a little bit like looking at a skeleton—she was trying to imagine the ship before the wreck.

"A pretty little schooner—three-masted sailboat," Stephen told the kids. "The wreck was in 1921."

"That old?" Louis said. "I can't believe it's still here!"

"It was mostly covered by sand for about fifty years—that protected it," his uncle explained. "The park service moved it into the shelter of these dunes in the 1970s so it could be displayed."

"In the spring and winter, when the ocean tears down the beaches, it still uncovers old wrecks," Megan added. "In the summer people lie on the beach and they have no idea all this stuff is buried under them."

"I thought I had to learn to scuba dive to hunt wrecks," Alex said. "Maybe I just need a shovel."

Stephen laughed. "I recommend the water," he said. "Much more fun. Speaking of which . . ." He gestured back the way they'd come.

"All right!" Ray exclaimed.

Alex and the others were already trotting in the soft sand toward the parking area and Stephen's boat.

They followed him in the Jeep down the ocean highway into the village of Buxton, where they stopped at a gas station and changed into their swimsuits.

Then they took a bumpy, unpaved road through a stand of trees to a small dock where the road ran into the water—a launch. Stephen backed the trailer into the water and they all waded in to push her off.

When the boat cleared the trailer, Alex climbed aboard and tossed a line to Louis, who wrapped it around a piling to hold the boat until the others could park the truck and the trailer.

Alex found she could bring the boat alongside the pilings by pulling on the dock line, so the others could come aboard from the dock.

They followed the shoreline to the end of the island and came around into a wide expanse of open water. "Oregon Inlet," Stephen said. "It's the way out of the sound, into the ocean."

Alex was surprised at how shallow it was. It seemed that if she could reach into the water she could run her fingers along the sandy bottom. "They have to constantly scoop the sand in the channel to keep it deep enough for larger boats," Stephen told her. "This used to be land, until a hurricane cut through. The name comes from the first ship that went through—the *Oregon*. It was so convenient that people have been working at keeping it open ever since."

When they got to the middle of the inlet the water changed. Before it had been flat and calm. Suddenly the boat was bouncing in choppy wavelets.

"Not a problem," Stephen shouted over the sound of the engine. "This is where the tide and the currents from the ocean meet the flow from the sound—sort of a running argument. It'll smooth out when we're out in the Atlantic." In a few minutes they were in slick water again. Off to the right they could see a line of breakers pounding against a sandy shoreline.

"That's Ocracoke Island," Stephen said. "People who live on that island have a very distinctive accent that goes back several hundred years. Call themselves 'High Tiders,' only they pronounce it 'Hoi Toiders.' "

They curved around the island and followed its shoreline a safe distance from the breakers until they made out a dark object on the water. At first Alex thought it was another boat—which it was, but not the kind she was thinking.

"Wreck number two," Stephen said. "The *Oriental*. Went down in 1862. Not very deep, though. That's part of her engine—the boiler— sticking up out of the water."

"I don't think we'll be needing air tanks for this dive," Alex said. They motored up to the wreck in the flat calm, cut the engine, and dropped an anchor a few yards from the boiler.

"That's right," Stephen said. "This is a snorkel trip. No air tanks, just a face mask, snorkel tube, and fins. Most of the time you'll just float on the surface and look down. If you want to touch, you go down for just as long as you can comfortably hold your breath."

Alex took a practice breath.

"It'll be under a minute," Stephen said. "Then you go back to a floating position, blow the air out of the snorkel, and start breathing again."

"What if we run out of air while we're down?" Ray wondered.

"As soon as you start to feel uncomfortable, just turn around and head back for the light. Don't panic—you'll have plenty of time," Stephen assured them. He moved to the stern.

"Never go inside the wreck," he warned them. "It's dark and muddy anyway, and you could get trapped."

After giving them a few seconds to think about it, Stephen went in to demonstrate proper snorkeling. He stepped off the back of the boat and splashed in. Then he stretched out on the surface facedown, floating and breathing calmly through his snorkel tube, surveying the wreck through his face mask.

All at once they heard him inhale and exhale sharply through the tube—once, twice, then a third time, this time holding it, a long deep breath.

Then he folded at the waist, lifted his fins straight up above the water, and sank like a stone. He was down for almost a minute before he broke the surface again near the anchor line.

"Great visibility, gang," he said, out of breath as if he'd been running. The mask made him sound as if he had a stuffy nose. "The water's nice and warm, too. And no current. Great conditions. Let me give you an orientation on the boat and then you can have at it."

He'd already asked them the day before, but Stephen checked again to make sure Ray and Alex knew how to swim. He suggested they do most of their observing from the surface, face-down in the water, breathing through their snorkel, as he had shown them.

"If you want to go down, the easy way is to use the anchor line, hand over hand. That's also a good way to come up, following the anchor line. That's how you'd do it if this were a deep dive. It helps you know where your boat is. And watch what you touch down there—wrecks have lots of sharp edges."

"See any sharks, Uncle Stephen?"

"Plenty of fish, but no, nothing like that," he said. "But that reminds me—don't reach inside the wreck. You could be barging in on somebody's house."

Finally they put on their gear and went into the water. Stephen kept a watchful eye on them from the boat.

Floating facedown in the water, looking at the wreck from above, Alex enjoyed a peaceful floating sensation. The water lapped around her ears, and her back was a little chilly, but for the most part it seemed dreamlike. Bars of sunlight bent by the ripples on the surface played over the greenish wreck. Fish glided over the vague shapes of the wreck that looked more like natural rock than anything man-made. When Alex went under to join them, she entered a silent world, wonderfully peaceful.

She wondered what it would be like to morph down here.

Suddenly the quiet was interrupted by a low drumming sound. The whole scene changed abruptly as the fish scattered to the shadow side of the wreck. As the drumming noise increased, Alex looked up and ascended toward the silvery surface.

PHEW! Alex used the air in her chest to blow water out of the snorkel tube. Then she opened her mouth and let the mouthpiece drop. Attached to her face mask by a rubber ring, the snorkel tube hung loosely by her face.

She felt the drumming noise in her whole body now. Turning toward it, she saw what it was—another powerboat passing.

Two people in dark wet suits each raised a hand to Stephen's boat as they passed. Wreck divers, with scuba gear, headed for one of the deeper wrecks. Their fingers were curled in the okay sign—the diver's signal meaning "Is everything all right?"

Stephen okayed back and the boat curved away, heading south.

"I wonder where they're going," Louis said. He was bobbing in the water about six feet from Alex.

"Just going out to pick up a few doubloons, pieces of eight, gold bars, stuff like that," Alex said, imitating the pirate in a local TV commercial.

"Hey, that's why I'm here," Louis kidded. And he pulled down his mask and lay on the surface to get ready for another treasure dive on the *Oriental.*

Alex had another ambition. Off in the distance she caught a glimpse of a tiny sail. She could just make out the shape of a person standing at the mast, gliding along with feet planted firmly on the deck at water level.

A boardsailer.

Now that looked like a lot of fun, too.

"Want a lesson?" Alex heard Megan say. She'd noticed Alex's attention on the sail in the distance.

Alex gave a grin. "How'd you know what I was thinking?" she asked.

Dinner that night was fresh seafood served on the huge weathered gray deck that lined the front of the cottage facing the ocean. After the long afternoon of swimming, Alex was famished. She could really go for a pizza or some thick burgers. But when she saw what was for dinner, her heart sank.

Fish. Alex didn't want to hurt the Driscolls' feelings, but she didn't really like fish that much. Back home, her mom sometimes cooked frozen fillets in the microwave—she said it was good for Dad's heart—but Alex usually didn't like it.

But she was starving. And her mom had always taught her that when she was a guest at a house it was polite at least to try what they served. So tentatively she used her fork to cut off a small piece and put it in her mouth. Her eyes widened in surprise. "This is good!" she exclaimed.

Megan and her family laughed.

"You seem surprised," Laura said.

"It doesn't taste like the fish my mom cooks back in Paradise Valley," Alex admitted, blushing slightly.

Uncle Stephen nodded. "I know what you mean. I wasn't a big seafood eater till I moved here. But this is fresh fish. I mean really fresh. It was probably caught this morning. That makes a difference."

"Try this," Aunt Laura said, passing her a napkin-lined basket. "It's fresh clam strips."

Alex knew she'd never eaten clams before, but these were delicious.

"Want some hush puppies?" Megan asked her, passing the breadbasket.

"Maybe," Alex said hesitantly, "if you tell me what they are."

"It's a deep-fried fritter," Laura explained. "The story goes that they were created by hunters or fishermen when they were out cooking over a campfire. It was easy to cook them over a campfire, and when the dogs came round begging for food, they'd toss them to the dogs and say, 'Hush, puppy.' "

"They sure work on people," Stephen joked.

"Hey, Dad," Megan asked between mouthfuls, "did you hear any more about that new shipwreck?"

"A new one?" Louis piped up. "Cool—can we go see it, Uncle Stephen?"

Stephen shook his head. "Not this one. The state archaeologists have just discovered a new shipwreck south of Ocracoke. Rumor has it that it might be one of Blackbeard's ships—Silver

Lake at the south end of the island was a known hideout of his."

"You mean Blackbeard the pirate?" Ray exclaimed.

"Do you know anybody else named Blackbeard?" Megan teased.

"But it's all being kept really quiet," Stephen explained. "Some state archaeologists came by today to tell me about the wreck—and to warn me away from the area."

"Really, Stephen?" Laura looked concerned. "What did they say?"

"They just want to make sure I'm not taking any dive trips out to the area," he said. "They're really trying to guard the site until they can determine exactly what they've found."

After dinner Stephen took the kids by the dive shop to check messages. He was expecting to hear from a group coming down from Teaneck, New Jersey.

Just then the little bell over the door rang and a blond-haired young man came in.

Alex froze. It was the guy she'd seen in the Elizabethan Gardens that morning! She jabbed Ray in the ribs.

"What, Alex?" Ray whispered.

"It's him," she tried to whisper. But Ray couldn't understand what she was saying.

Before she could say anything else, she heard Stephen say something even more startling.

"Hey, Nick! Come on in. I'd like you to meet my nephew and his friends."

Stephen Driscoll knows this guy?

"Gang, this is Nick Stoll—he works for me here at the shop," Stephen said. "I sort of inherited him from the previous owner, isn't that right, Nick?"

"Kind of like the barnacle that won't wash off," he joked.

"No, you're a great help to me, Nick," Stephen told him. "I wouldn't know what I was doing around here if it weren't for you."

"Well, okay, if you say so—you're the boss!" He laughed. Here in the dive shop, Nick seemed friendly and agreeable. Nothing like he was in the gardens—tough and aggressive.

Then Louis spotted a shipwreck map hanging on the wall, which gave the locations and names of over a hundred shipwrecks that had been charted along the coast of North Carolina. Originally published in *National Geographic*, it had become a favorite among tourists. "Hey, this is cool. Do you guys sell these?"

"Sure," Megan said. "Want one?"

"You bet."

"Me, too," Ray added.

Alex wanted one, too. It would make a nice souvenir framed on her wall back home.

Ray and Louis gathered around Megan as she dug through a bin of maps and posters that the shop had for sale. But just then something Stephen was saying to Nick Stoll caught her attention.

"Say, Nick," Stephen said, flipping through his record books behind the counter, "did you forget to log in your divers yesterday?"

"What divers?" Nick responded casually as he grabbed a pack of peanuts from the snack shelf and ripped open the cellophane.

Stephen rubbed the back of his neck. "Maybe I've got the days mixed up, you know me, but I could have sworn you took the boat out yesterday."

"Oh, those." Nick scratched his ear, squinting and covering his facial expression. "Those were just friends of mine, not paying customers. It wasn't a dive or anything. So I didn't bother making a record."

Alex noticed that Stephen looked a little embarrassed, but went ahead and said, "Well, I hate to stir things up from how you guys used to do it, but, well, how about from now on we log in all trips." He shrugged good-naturedly. "You know, just to keep things tidy. Especially with the state guys worried about the shipwreck."

Nick tossed another handful of peanuts into his mouth and shrugged. "No problem." Then he swung his gaze toward Alex and she nearly jumped.

It was nerve-racking. She didn't feel sure he hadn't caught a glimpse of her in the gardens this morning.

But all he said was, "See y'all later."

"Yeah, nice to meet you, Mr. Stoll," Louis replied with a wave.

But as Alex watched the handsome diver stroll out of the dive shop, she couldn't help feeling that something was not right with him.

*   *   *

That night, when she and Megan got ready for bed, Alex tried to ask her some questions about Nick Stoll.

"Nick?" Megan said as she slipped into her bed. "He's really great. Dad says he's really lucky to have him. I mean, Dad's been diving since he was a teenager, but he doesn't know much about running a business. Nick's really helped him get the hang of how the shop operates." She leaned closer over her pillow and grinned. "Actually, I had kind of a crush on him when I first got here," she admitted. "I mean, who wouldn't? He's so cute, and funny, and just really nice to everybody . . ." She sighed when she saw Alex's look of surprise. "I know, I know, he's way too old for me," she said with a laugh. Then she peered at Alex with a teasing glint in her eye. "Why all the questions, Alex? Don't tell me you've got the hots for Nick Stoll, too?"

"No way," Alex said emphatically. "He's not my type."

"What—cute and charming?" Megan said. "So what is your type—rude and ugly?"

Alex responded by tossing her down pillow at

Megan's bed, prompting a pillow fight that raged until Megan's mom came to the door and told them lights out.

So Nick is a charmer, Alex thought. Cute, too—she'd noticed that.

She hoped Megan was right. Maybe she was imagining things.

CHAPTER 4

The next morning at breakfast Laura laid out a combination of northern bagels and southern biscuits, complete with a large selection of cream cheese, butter, and local homemade jellies and jams. Alex loved bagels, but biscuits were an alien bread form, and she decided to try one, slathered with butter.

"Mmmm," she exclaimed as she bit into the fluffy, flaky biscuit. "This is delicious. Did you make these, Laura?"

"Uh-huh. A neighbor down the street taught me how to make them. It's her great-grandmother's recipe." She broke one open and steam rose from its fluffy innards. "This alone was worth moving to the South!" she said with a laugh.

"So where are Dad and Louis?" Megan asked her mom.

"They got up early to take a dip in the ocean," Laura explained, then grinned at Ray. "Louis said he tried to wake you up, Ray . . ."

"No problem," Ray said. "Sleeping in is my favorite vacation activity."

The phone by the kitchen counter rang and Laura answered. It was Stephen.

"Hang on, I'll check," Laura said. She went to the front door where the Driscolls kept keys in a small wooden cabinet on the wall. She removed a ring with a small silver key and took it back to the phone. "It's here. Do you want somebody to bring it over? Okay, no problem."

Then she hung up and asked Megan if she wanted to take a trip over to the shop. Stephen needed the key to the powerboat—he'd left it at the house from their wreck hunt the day before.

"Meet me at the shop later," Megan said to Alex and Ray on her way out with Laura.

Alex was only barely aware of the morning

small talk; she couldn't stop thinking about Nick and the conversation in the Elizabethan Gardens. It was like a puzzle. The pieces were all in front of her—now if she could only fit them together.

There's definitely something fishy going on, she thought. . . .

That's it! she suddenly realized, and she pulled Ray away from the little TV in the kitchen.

Ray was so wrapped up in an ad he'd just seen he couldn't stop laughing.

"This is important, Ray," she said.

"Uh-huh," he said, still laughing from the ad for the TV show.

"Ray, please pay attention," Alex said.

"I am, I am," he assured her.

Alex could see his eyes were still moist from laughing. She could tell he was trying, though.

"Go on, shoot," Ray said. " 'Sup?"

"Ray," Alex said, "I've been thinking about Nick Stoll all night."

"Why, hey, Al," he teased. "You weren't kidding when you said be serious, were you? But I didn't think you went for blonds."

Alex rolled her eyes at her best friend. "Ray, I'm serious! I've been putting two and two together. What I heard in the garden tells me Nick is up to something illegal. Something that someone *else* is willing to pay for.

"Think about it," she insisted. "What does Nick do for money?" Alex paused and let it sink in.

"Dive?" Ray guessed.

"Right!" Alex said. "And what kind of diving is illegal right now?" She didn't wait for Ray to answer. "Diving on that historical wreck everybody's talking about! I think maybe what I overheard in the gardens was Nick selling stuff from the shipwreck!"

"Alex," Ray said, "have you been reading your mom's detective novels again? Your imagination is running away with you."

"I'm not kidding, Ray," Alex insisted. "It makes sense. And Nick said it was just the warm-up. If I'm right, he's been going back for more, and he'll keep going back until somebody stops him."

"Okay, okay," Ray told her, putting his hands up in front of him. "I believe you. I guess. But maybe you should just forget about it. It really hasn't got anything to do with you."

"How can you say that?" Alex whispered, glancing over her shoulder at her host. "What if he is doing something illegal? And what if it gets Stephen and Laura in trouble?"

"Hmm," Ray said. "I hadn't thought of that."

"Do you think I ought to tell Stephen?" Alex asked.

"Maybe," Ray said. "But, Al, you don't have any proof of anything. All you can say is that you overheard what you think these guys said. It's their word against yours. And what if it's nothing?"

"I guess you're right." Then Alex had another horrible thought. "Oh, no! You don't think Stephen is in on it, too, do you? What if I start asking questions and get Stephen in trouble? Poor Megan. Poor Louis!"

"Hold on, Alex," Ray said. "Stephen seems like too nice a guy to get mixed up in something like that."

Just then Louis, his uncle Stephen, and his aunt Laura returned from the shop with newspapers under their arms. They dropped them onto the kitchen table in front of Alex: the *Virginian-*

Pilot out of Norfolk, plus a local weekly and a free tabloid shopper.

"Help yourself to those," Stephen said. He and Laura were leaving early for an appointment with a bank officer about a small loan for the business. The bank wasn't open yet, but in Nags Head it wasn't unusual for a breakfast table at one of the local restaurants to serve as a temporary business office. Megan was minding the shop during the meeting.

Ray sat down at the table and glanced at the papers.

"Okay, later," Louis said. He was staring into the open refrigerator, looking for a follow-up to breakfast. When his aunt and uncle were gone, Louis came out with two slices of bread and went to a cabinet for peanut butter.

"Guess what?" Louis exclaimed as he sat down at the table with Alex and Ray. "We saw some porpoises out in the surf this morning. It was awesome!" he said.

Between bites of peanut butter sandwich, Louis described the way the animals played in the surf, not noticing that neither Ray nor Alex was paying much attention.

Ray was reading the front page of the local paper.

Alex was wondering why Ray's eyes were bulging like that.

She didn't have to ask.

"Uh, Alex," Ray whispered, "I just discovered another reason you don't want to report the conversation you overheard in the gardens yesterday."

"Really?" she asked. "What?"

Ray slid the newspaper across the table for Alex to see. A big news story on the front page caught her eye. It was about a young local amateur videographer. He'd made an unusual videotape in the Elizabethan Gardens early the morning before.

Louis came over to see what could be more important than his story about the porpoises.

"Whoa, get this!" he exclaimed, grabbing the paper out from under Alex's nose before she could get a good look. "This guy says he has a video of the ghost of Virginia Dare!"

Louis began to read out loud: "Local resident Henry Crompton was making a video in the Elizabethan Gardens about nine o'clock in the morning . . ."

He must have been the tourist I saw after I morphed, Alex thought.

"According to Crompton, 'I spotted the most amazing thing through my viewfinder. An image of a young girl, with long hair, darting through the bushes. At first I thought she was just another tourist, but then, before my eyes, she faded into the mist. Like a ghost. I knew it must be her—Virginia Dare. And she looked as if she were searching for someone.'

"It is not the first time someone has claimed to see the ghost of a teenage Virginia Dare in the gardens, and many folklorists like to say it's her ghost, returning with news of the Lost Colony. But it is the first time anyone has claimed to have a video of the event."

"Hey, Alex," Louis said as he passed the paper to Ray, "you were there yesterday morning. Did you see any ghosts wandering around?"

"No," Alex said emphatically.

But then she noticed the worried look on Ray's face as he held out the newspaper to her.

There was a high-school photo of Henry Crompton, a harmless-looking teenager with a goofy grin on his face.

And next to that, another photo—a still from Henry Crompton's video.

Yikes! Alex thought. She wasn't a ghost hunter. And she knew only a little about North Carolina history.

But one thing she was sure of. That wasn't the ghost of Virginia Dare disappearing in the morning mist.

It's a picture of me—in the middle of a morph!

CHAPTER 5

"Ray," Alex whispered as Louis went into his room to grab a T-shirt. "That's me—morphing! On the front page!"

"I know, I know!" Ray whispered, glancing around to make sure Louis hadn't heard. "This is really bad news!"

"Do you think anybody could recognize me?" Alex asked. If they could, she'd have a really hard time explaining this.

Ray peered at the photograph. "I don't know, Al. The photo's pretty blurry."

"Yeah, you're right," Alex said nervously. "And nobody around here knows me anyway— except the Driscolls."

Ray nodded. "Folks will probably just think this guy is nuts—or a bad photographer. Nobody'll believe his story."

"I'm ready, guys," Louis said, coming into the kitchen. "Time to boogie!"

Alex had to laugh at her friend. He was wearing a T-shirt that said: CHAIRMAN OF THE (BOOGIE) BOARD.

"Hey, I'm ready, too!" Ray said, flashing his famous dazzling smile. He pretended to listen to something, then sighed in delight. "I hear the ocean calling my name."

First they cleaned up the breakfast table and put the dishes in the dishwasher. Then they dashed for the door that led to the ocean-facing deck.

Just then they heard a knock at the front door.

"Hold on, guys," Alex said, turning around. "I'd better see who that is." She hurried across the living area and flung open the front door.

A tall thin guy with thick dark hair and startling blue eyes smiled at her. "You must be Alex Mack!"

Alex gasped. It was Henry Crompton—the ghost hunter from the newspaper article!

How did he track me down here? she wondered frantically.

And more important, *How does he know my name?*

Just then Ray came up behind her, his brown eyes wide in surprise.

"And you must be Ray," the teenager went on as he stuck out his hand. "I'm Henry Crompton."

Alex and Ray stared openmouthed at him.

Henry looked around. "Is Megan here?"

"Y-you know Megan?" Alex managed to stutter.

A blush stole across Henry's tanned face. "Sure, I guess I oughta. I mean, she's sort of my, um, girlfriend."

"She is?" Ray asked.

Henry nodded. "She told me y'all were coming to visit with her cousin Louis."

"That's me," Louis said, coming up behind Ray.

"Nice to meet you," Henry said. "So, is Megan here?" He held up a newspaper he'd been holding under one arm, smiling rather proudly. "I came by to show her the big write-up about me in this morning's paper."

Alex fell back against Ray, nearly collapsing in relief. Henry Crompton hadn't tracked her down. And he didn't seem to make any connection between the fuzzy picture in the video and her face in real life.

She just hoped it stayed that way!

"Um, Megan's not here," Ray said, giving Alex's hand a reassuring squeeze. "She told us to meet her down at the dive shop. That's where we're headed now."

"Great," Henry said, following them out of the house.

That was one thing Alex really liked about the Outer Banks. Practically everything on the island was arranged along one main road running parallel to the beach. So there were two ways to get anywhere you wanted to go—take the road, or take the beach. Of course, they did most of their traveling on the sand route.

They even had their choice among sand that was warm, medium, or cool—the high dry sand was warm, the dark wet sand was cool, and everything in between was in between.

"So how do you like it here?" Henry asked. "Is it your first time here? When a local wants to get from point A to point B he generally takes the street. It's faster."

Alex took in a deep breath of fresh salty air. "But not as beautiful. I feel so healthy here."

"And it's not as crowded as some of the beaches I've been to," Ray added. He leaped up to catch a Frisbee that had gone astray, then flung it back to one of the guys in the game.

"Thanks, man!" the kid called out.

"Well, you should have seen it when I was a kid," Henry said. "It was practically deserted compared to this. It's really grown a lot since then."

Alex didn't think Henry had been alive long enough to see *that* much happen. "Like, how long ago are we talking about?" she asked.

"Oh, years and years," Henry said. "Like since I was two or three. I remember stuff from back then—it was very different, believe me."

I just hope he can't remember too much from yesterday! Alex thought.

They could see Graveyard Divers from the beach—it was one of several businesses that shared a small shopping center that was on the ocean side of the beach road. The part of the building that faced the ocean included shops that catered to tourists who were using the beach: an ice-cream store, a surf shop, and a place for sunglasses. The dive shop was on the other side of the building, but Stephen kept a flag flying—the "Diver Down" flag, red with a diagonal white stripe, that was normally flown out on the water to warn boaters that a diver was below in the area.

They trudged up the deep sand to the shop, and Megan came running out. "Hi, Henry!" she called out happily. "What's new?"

Henry beamed as he held out one of the papers. "Me!"

Megan smiled in delight to see her boyfriend's face on the front page, then quickly scanned the article. Suddenly she burst out laughing. "Oh, Henry, you're kidding! The ghost of Virginia Dare?"

Henry shrugged. This was obviously not the reception he'd expected from the girl who was supposed to adore him.

"Who knows? It could be her," he insisted. "My great-grandfather always swore he saw her ghost once."

"But what was she doing there in the morning?" Megan argued. "Don't ghosts just come out at night?"

"How do I know?!" Henry's face was turning red now. "I'm not an expert on ghosts—I just know I saw something. Got it on tape, I mean!"

Alex and Ray shifted uncomfortably. Louis seemed oblivious to the fact that an argument was brewing.

But then Megan just laughed and slipped her arm through Henry's. "Come on, Henry. Don't get upset. We believe you"—she giggled—"don't we, guys?"

"Sure," Louis said. "This is a very historical place. I bet the whole island's crawling with ghosts!"

Then he took Henry's other arm and said in a confidential tone, "Say, Henry, have you made any plans yet?"

Henry looked confused. "Uh, about what, Louis?"

Louis rolled his eyes. "For the tape! What else? You know, you could probably sell this to one of those hot news programs—you know, the ones that are always doing stories on UFOs and stuff?"

"Really?" Henry said. The hurt expression was fading. His normal dreamy, in-a-fog kind of look was coming back.

"Oh, absolutely!" Louis assured him. "I bet they'd pay a lot for a tape like yours."

Henry was really glowing now. "You know, I could use a nice contribution to my college fund. Maybe I'll think about it. But I really don't know how to go about it."

"Leave it to me, pal," Louis said. "What you need is an agent—somebody who's had experience with these things. Somebody who'll shop your video around for the highest bid."

"Like who?" Megan asked.

Louis grinned. "Hey! Like me!"

Alex and Ray burst into laughter. They'd have to warn Henry about their good friend Louis.

"You know that place where we put the boat in yesterday? It was by a place called Canadian Hole. If there had been any wind you'd have seen a dozen sailboards out there." Megan and Alex were on Highway 24 again, heading south in the Jeep toward Buxton.

Two sailboards hung over the tailgate—Alex was about to get her first sailboarding lesson from Megan.

"You know, I just love trying new things," Alex

said, leaning back in the seat to enjoy the ride. The sky overhead was cloudless blue. "I remember learning how to ride a bicycle for the first time. I was just barely big enough to reach the pedals."

"How'd it go?" Megan asked.

"I think I remember my dad commenting on all the bandages we were going through." Alex laughed.

"Well, you probably won't skin your knees learning to sail," Megan commented. "But be prepared to get very wet."

Just before they reached the town of Buxton, Megan turned off and headed for the sound.

The water was glassy under a light puffy wind.

Alex and Megan put the sailboards down on a small grassy beach by a cove on the edge of the sound. They saw in the distance a pair of pretty sails—a triangle with red-and-white stripes and another light green—skimming over the blue water. Alex sat down and watched.

Then it was time for the lesson.

"First of all," Megan said, "the thing you're sitting on is called the board."

"The surfboard," Alex said.

"Sailboard," Megan said. "The main difference between a sailboard and a surfboard is the thing in the center." She dragged the bottom of a long pole to the metal fitting in the center of the board. "It's called a *universal.*

"The pole that attaches to the universal is the *mast.* The other pole, the one that comes out the side of the mast, is called the *boom.* When the mast is up, it and the boom hold the sail along two of its edges."

"Basically like a sailboat, right?" Alex asked.

"Sort of," Megan said. "The difference is, on a sailboat, the mast stays straight up and down in the boat. If a sailboat was sitting by the dock, and you went over and pulled on the mast, the whole boat would tilt with it."

"That makes sense," Alex said.

"But the mast on a sailboard is different," Megan went on. "On a sail*board*, the mast is supposed to tilt back and forth—the universal lets it do that. Which way you tilt the mast decides which way you go." Megan lifted the mast and put one foot on the board. The other foot stayed on the ground to keep everything steady.

"Tilt the mast forward," Megan said, leaning a little to the left, "and the board will turn you away from the wind. You'll sail with the wind behind you."

"Got it," Alex said.

Then Megan bent a little to the right, leaning the mast back toward the rear of the board. "Tilt the mast back," she said, "and the board will turn you upwind. You'll sail into the wind."

"And what if the mast is straight up and down?"

"With the mast straight up and down you sail across the wind. We'll try that first." Megan turned and faced the wind. "Nice gentle wind out of the south," she said. "That's why it's so warm. Great day for a first lesson."

They scooted one of the sailboards into the water with the mast up. As soon as they were a few yards from the trees the sail bulged with air and Alex could feel the mast want to tip over. She automatically put a foot on the board to balance it.

"Go ahead and get on," Megan said. "Once the sail fills I won't be able to hold it up. Grab the boom and lean back a little until you feel balanced, and enjoy the ride!"

Alex stepped onto the board and concentrated on finding the right pose to steady herself on the board. At first Alex didn't realize that Megan had let go. She didn't even realize she'd been moving until she looked back and saw Megan standing about twenty feet behind her.

Alex was so stunned she threw her head back and—

SPLASH! She pulled the sailboard down on top of her.

"Good job!" Megan yelled. "Really great! You did it!"

Alex picked herself up, lifted the mast, rolling water off the sail, felt the wind, and hopped on again.

This time she almost went over the other way, sail first, but managed to rock back in time and stay upright.

And she went a long way until she tried to turn, when she splashed down again.

"You're getting the hang of it now!" Megan yelled in the distance. She'd gone back to the beach for the other board.

In a few minutes they were out together on the sound. Alex was a little shaky, and felt like she was spending about half the time swimming, but she was getting the hang of it. As long as she could go straight, she was fine. And whenever she wanted a break, the water was shallow enough to stand in. Where they were sailing it was only about three feet deep.

She was standing on the bottom when she spotted the kayakers. Spotted them second—first she *heard* them, whooping it up for anyone who cared to notice, as well as anyone who didn't. The fact that they were upwind helped the sound of their joking carry.

Ray and Louis.

One behind the other in long yellow kayaks, they were heading straight for Alex. But they weren't paddling. They had their paddles raised overhead as if they were lifting barbells.

"Wooooooo!" Louis hooted.

"Check it out! Check it out!" Ray shouted insistently. He jabbed his paddle at the sky. "Up in the air! Look, Alex!"

Alex made a visor with her hand and squinted in the direction Ray was pointing. High over the water a short distance ahead of their kayaks a triangular kite sailed. She saw a flash of light as the sun struck the kite line that connected it to the bow of Ray's kayak. They were using the kite to pull them along for a free ride!

"Tell you what, Alex!" Ray laughed. "This kayaking is hard work! I see you're getting rested up, at least!"

Alex shook her head. They'd get their exercise on the way back. Paddling against the wind. Unlike a boardsail, kites and kayaks couldn't use the wind when it was going the wrong way.

"What do you say we go in for a little lunch on the beach," Megan suggested. "I packed some sandwiches."

"Yeah, we can watch for the return of Louis and . . ." Alex started to say—

"Louis and Clark!" they said at once and burst out laughing.

CHAPTER 6

"What in the world—?" Megan exclaimed when they got back to the dive shop late that afternoon.

The front door was locked. The sign in the window had been flipped over to read CLOSED.

Worried, Megan looked in through the window and tapped on the glass. "Dad? Dad! Are you in there?"

No one answered. The shop seemed deserted.

"What's the matter, Megan?" Alex asked her friend. She seemed really upset.

"Dad never closes up early," Megan explained. "He loves this place—he practically lives here."

"Maybe he just stepped out," Louis suggested.

"Yeah," Alex agreed. "Maybe he had to run an errand or something."

Megan shook her head. "He rarely locks up if he's just gone for a few minutes. Usually Nick or one of the other guys is around."

"Hey, I'm sure everything's okay," Henry tried to reassure her. "Come on, let's go to your house. Maybe your dad's there."

When they got to the Driscolls' cottage and went inside, they could see Megan's dad pacing up and down on the deck with a glass of iced tea in his hand. Laura seemed to be trying to calm him down.

Megan pushed open the sliding glass doors and hurried onto the deck. "Dad! What's wrong? Why's the shop closed?"

Alex and the others stayed inside, but they could hear everything the Driscoll family was saying.

Stephen Driscoll turned around and tried to smile at his daughter. "Hi, honey. Did you and your friends have a nice afternoon?"

"Mom, what's going on?"

"It's nothing, really, sweetheart," Laura said,

reaching out for her daughter's hand. "It's just, well—"

"They've shut me down!" Stephen exclaimed. "I can't—"

"Shut you down!" Louis stepped out onto the deck. "Uncle Stephen, what happened?"

Laura smiled at her nephew. "It's no big deal—"

"No big deal?" Stephen exclaimed hotly. "They shut down my business!"

"Just for a day or two," Laura pointed out. Then she turned to the kids. "Apparently there's been some more illegal diving at the shipwreck site. And the authorities have decided to place a moratorium on all diving until—"

"Until further notice," Stephen cut in. "Who knows when that will be."

"Now, Stephen, be fair," Laura said. "First of all they asked you to comply—it wasn't a direct order."

"Yeah," Stephen said. "But what was I supposed to say? No? Then they'd have shut me down."

"Well, there's nothing we can do about it," Laura said logically. "We'll just have to make the best of it. Hey, we can use this time to catch up on some of that paperwork. Or just to take it easy. You haven't taken a day of vacation since we moved out here, Stephen. You could use the break."

"But think of the business we'll lose!" Stephen said.

Graveyard Divers not only ran daily charters with its own boat, Megan explained to her friends, it had contracts with half a dozen other captains who ran daily trips to the wrecks. In the warm months, the boats went out two, sometimes three, times a day on weekends. The Driscolls' business depended on getting a small percentage of the boat fee for every diver that signed up for a trip through the shop. Plus the equipment rentals and air fill fees—they couldn't pay the rent for long just selling T-shirts.

Alex, Ray, Louis, and Henry followed Megan along the wooden-plank sidewalk that led to the beach. At the end of the walk they stopped to hang out in the small wooden gazebo with bench seats that sat amid the dunes.

Megan stared out at the ocean, the wind blowing her sun-streaked hair. "This isn't fair to Dad," she mumbled. "He's just getting started out here—and summer's his big season. It makes me so mad! I wish there was something I could do to help him."

Alex shot a glance at Ray. "Maybe there is," she said.

Megan, Henry, and Louis turned to stare at Alex.

"What do you mean?" Megan asked.

"Well . . ." She glanced sideways at Ray, asking her longtime best friend the silent question: *Should I tell her?*

Ray shrugged, then nodded. *Why not?*

Alex wasn't sure how to proceed. Megan—and just about everybody—really seemed to like Nick. If she was wrong about him, she might alienate her new friends, the Driscolls. But if she was right . . .

"Well," Alex began slowly, playing with the strap of her flipflop, "you're probably not going to like hearing this—"

"What?" Megan asked, sitting down next to Alex. "If it will help my dad . . ."

"It might," Alex said. She looked into Megan's bright green eyes and took a deep breath. "Well, you know when I was in the Elizabethan Gardens yesterday morning?''

''You were there, too?'' Henry asked. ''I didn't see you.''

''Well, it's a big garden,'' Alex said.

''Did you see the ghost?'' Louis wanted to know.

''No,'' Alex said. *Still time to back out*, she told herself. ''But I did see somebody else . . .'' Then she took a deep breath and told the breathless group of kids about seeing Nick and overhearing his conversation with the man working for Mr. K.

At first Megan jumped to her feet, shaking her head. ''I'm sorry, Alex, but you must have misunderstood. Nick's a great guy. He wouldn't do anything like that. I'm sure of it! I . . .''

Then she saw the looks passing between the other kids.

''He *did* know about the shipwreck before anybody else,'' Louis said. ''I heard him brag about it in the shop.''

''He *is* an experienced diver,'' Henry said. ''Plus, he's lived out here all his life, so he really knows these waters.''

Alex could tell that her friend didn't want to believe her dad's employee could be the one responsible for getting the dive shop shut down.

"He can't be involved," Megan insisted. Then she glanced back toward the house, where they could still see Stephen and Laura talking. "But what if he is?" she whispered mournfully. "What if he is?"

Alex slipped an arm around her new friend's shoulder. "Don't worry. We'll figure a way to get to the bottom of this."

Megan flashed her a grateful smile. "So, what do we do?"

The five kids went into a huddle. "Maybe we can figure out some way to catch Nick with the stuff," Ray suggested. "You know, follow him, or set some kind of trap."

"It shouldn't be hard," Louis said, growing more excited by the minute. "If Nick's diving for artifacts offshore, the goods must be in his boat when he docks."

"Wait a minute," Ray interrupted. "I don't understand. If these guys with the state are trying to protect the ship, how come they don't just catch him when he goes in?"

"Even if they have a watch out over the wreck," Megan explained, "which I don't think they do—not twenty-four hours a day, any-way—it's possible that a good diver could sal-vage a deep wreck without getting caught. He could go at night." She nodded to herself. "Somebody like Nick could probably squeeze a couple of hours of bottom time out of one night's work. If the wreck is really exposed, that's plenty of time to make a good haul. Once he found a good spot, he could mark it, just keep coming back, digging it like a mine . . ."

"Hey, we don't know anything until we have some evidence," Louis said. Then he slapped Henry on the back. "Which is why we're so lucky to have among us the man with the magic camera!"

CHAPTER 7

"But we don't want a refund!"

The next morning when Alex, Megan, Louis, and Ray met Henry at the dive shop, they found a group of five men who'd shown up for a dive trip arguing with Megan's dad.

"Oh, *man!* I am *bummed!*" a member of the group said. He wore a baseball cap that said: PARTY, PARTY, WHERE'S THE PARTY? It was outfitted with a tiny battery-powered orange plastic fan that was intended to help him keep his cool—but apparently it wasn't working.

"Look, Stephen. We want to dive. We came all the way from Teaneck, and we're only down here for a week."

"Listen, I'm really sorry, guys," Stephen Driscoll was apologizing to his customers. "My guy Nick was supposed to call you all last night and let you know the trip was canceled."

"Yeah, well, he didn't," a big guy answered.

"Well, I'm sorry," Stephen repeated. "But as you can tell from the sign it's not my doing. The state's placed a temporary moratorium on all diving along the coast till they can figure out a way to secure that new shipwreck discovery. It's out of my hands."

"Yeah, well . . ." The customer was obviously unhappy that he didn't have anybody he could justifiably yell at.

"Listen," Stephen told them, "you'll get a full refund of your deposit. And I'll tell you what. Make sure you leave me a number where I can reach you. And if things open back up before the week's out, I'll give you a ten percent discount if you want to reschedule your trip."

"Well," one of the men said reluctantly, "I guess that would do." He scribbled down a name and phone number, then grumbled to his friends, "Come on, guys, let's hit the pier and do some fishing."

When the customers had left, Megan hurried over to Stephen and gave him a quick hug. "Tough day, huh, Dad?"

"You ain't kidding," Stephen said, running a hand through his dark hair. "I've had to cancel several dive trips. And most of them are tourists who're only here for a brief stay. They don't care whose fault it is—I'm the one they want to blame."

"Hang in there, Uncle Stephen," Louis told his uncle. "I'm sure they'll get everything back to normal soon."

"I sure hope so." He flipped through his reservations book, and made a notation of the last customer's phone number. Then he glanced up at the kids with a big smile. "But, hey, don't let this stuff worry you guys. What have you got planned for today?"

"Well," Megan said, shooting a glance at Alex, "the guys wanted to see the marina where you keep the dive boats. Any chance we could get a quick tour?"

"Sure," Stephen said, closing his reservations book. "I need to talk to somebody down at Hattie's near Buxton—it's a long trip but it's not like I've got a whole lot to do around here."

The kids walked outside, and Stephen locked up, after making sure the sign about the state-ordered dive ban was clear in the window.

"Listen, I'll take the pickup and meet you there," Stephen said. "I may want to stay there awhile, and if Megan takes the Jeep, then you guys can leave if you get bored."

Louis rode with his uncle, while Alex, Ray, and Henry piled into the Jeep with Megan. They took the highway in the direction of Hatteras and the long drive down the national seashore to the marina where Megan knew Nick kept a small boat.

They knew they were getting close when they saw a van-filled beach-access parking area. Surfers. They were at Cape Point, a major East Coast attraction for waves.

"I can't believe how narrow the island is here," Alex exclaimed. In some places the land looked only about a mile from ocean to sound.

"Sometimes when there are huge storms, this road can get washed out," Henry said.

At last they came to the turn-in for Hattie's Marina.

They followed a dirt road packed hard by trailered-boat traffic using the marina's ramp access to the sound. The marina office was also the owner's living quarters—a trailer home with a business office in the living room. A drive-through window was installed in the end of the unit for curb service. It even had a window box of flowers.

A cheerful sign in the window notified anyone who wanted to know that the owner was out.

BE BACK SOMETIME . . .

LIFE'S A BEACH—HAVE A NICE DAY!

Megan parked the Jeep by the trailer rather than drive to the docks and risk catching Nick's attention.

He noticed them right away.

"Hey, y'all!" he hollered. Seeing Henry, he added, "You guys makin' a movie?"

Alex was mortified. Nick was in the middle of giving a boat named *Not Guilty* a cleanup.

Henry waved and smiled and wagged his camera. He had become something of a local celebrity. Following his example, Alex waved and smiled confidently.

"Just showing Alex and Ray around," Megan called out.

It seemed to work. Nick waved his towel and went right back to work. Alex frowned. There was absolutely nothing suspicious about his behavior. *You'd think if he was stealing artifacts, he'd look more nervous,* Alex thought. *But then, maybe to be a good thief you have to be a good actor.*

Megan showed them a boat not far from the one Nick was working on. "If only we could get on the boat and look around," Alex whispered in Ray's ear. "Without Nick around."

But there didn't seem to be any way of doing that. Nick seemed glued to the boat, with no sign of leaving anytime soon.

They heard gravel crunch behind them. It was Stephen and Louis.

"Say, listen, Nick," Stephen said as he moved up to Nick's boat. "Would you mind coming by the house this evening?"

Alex noticed that a slight frown crossed Nick's brow, before he relaxed his face into a smile. "Well, I sort of had some plans . . ."

"Are they important?" Stephen asked. "There are some things on the books I really need to go over with you. I don't think we should let 'em slide."

Nick shrugged. "Well, sure then. No problem. I could come by for a little while. Around eight maybe?"

Stephen grinned. "Sounds good. See you then."

"I'll see you guys for dinner," Stephen told Megan and her friends. Then he climbed into his pickup and drove off.

Louis stayed behind. He had come up with a good excuse in case they needed to hang around the marina awhile—a fishing rod borrowed from his uncle's truck. The others got sodas from the machine outside Hattie's trailer and watched Louis fish without any bait.

But soon it became obvious that Nick wasn't leaving—at least not anytime soon.

"This is a waste of time," Louis said finally, reeling in his line. "We might as well go do something fun."

"But what about Nick?" Megan complained. "I've got to know if he's up to something."

"Why don't we all come back at night?" Louis suggested. "When we know Nick's going to be at Uncle Stephen's? Then maybe we can sneak on the boat and check it out."

Alex had to admit to herself that Louis's naturally devious mind did occasionally come in handy.

But she didn't miss the shiver that went down her spine at the thought of sneaking around here after dark.

That evening, dinner at the Driscolls' was tacos on the deck, with a batch of homemade peach ice cream cranked out in the old-fashioned, hand-cranked ice-cream freezer using peaches Laura had bought at a roadside stand. Alex had to admit it was the most delicious ice cream she'd ever tasted. "Maybe you should add an ice-cream parlor to the dive shop," Alex suggested, licking her spoon.

"We may have to if they don't reopen the diving soon," Stephen said glumly. But when Laura gave him a jab with her elbow, he brightened. "Hey, maybe we could try watermelon ice cream. Think that would sell?"

The kids were evenly divided between "Yum" and "Gross" on that suggestion, and they spent the next few minutes trying to dream up the best new ice-cream flavors. Alex got the most votes with pineapple-banana.

"If I can find a fresh pineapple, we'll try that while you're here," Laura promised.

Nervously watching the clock, the kids cleaned up, while Stephen and Laura sat on the deck and watched the beach scene clear out as couples and families took their after-dinner strolls along the shoreline.

"Okay, so where is he?" Megan asked, scrubbing the already clean countertops.

Just then headlights flashed along the front of the cottage, and Alex went to the window. "He's here!" she whispered loudly. "Get ready, everybody!"

In a few seconds they heard Megan let Nick in. "Hello, Megan. Hello, kids. Nice to see y'all again. Is your dad home, honey?"

Alex saw her friend bristle, but Megan just smiled and said, "Sure, he and Mom are out on the deck." She led him out there.

Then Alex heard her tell her parents, "Mom, Dad, is it okay if we go out? We might go see a movie."

"Sure, sweetheart," her mom said. "Who's driving?"

"Henry," Megan said.

"Fine," Laura said. "Henry's the best driver I

know. But you guys be careful, and don't stay out too late, okay?"

"Sure, Mom, we'll be home in time for a second helping of that ice cream," Megan said. She sounded cheerful, but Alex could tell it was forced.

Alex knew they should let the Driscolls know where they were going. But wouldn't that cause problems between Nick and Stephen? They still weren't sure—and Stephen and Laura had enough on their minds already, Alex told herself.

And then they were all bustling out of the house and into Henry's '72 Volkswagen bus.

"Wow, Henry, this is a cool vehicle!" Ray exclaimed, sliding open the side door.

"Hey, look!" Alex said. "It's even got a sink and a fridge. This is awesome!"

"It's a VW camper," Henry explained as he buckled his seat belt. "My dad and I are restoring it."

Soon they were heading down the highway toward Bodie Island.

Megan seemed to be staring out the front window without talking. Alex reached up and patted her friend on the shoulder. "Did you feel weird telling your mom we were going to the movies?"

"Well, you noticed I just said we *might* go see a movie," Megan pointed out. "But, yeah, my parents are pretty cool, and I'm usually pretty straight with them about everything. But this is important. This is to help Dad."

Henry patted Megan on the shoulder. "Don't worry. If we get done with this soon, maybe I'll still take you guys to a movie. How about that?"

Megan laughed nervously. "I feel like I'm in a movie tonight."

Alex shivered a little. She had to agree.

The sun was just sinking below the horizon when they arrived at the marina and parked. There was a clubhouse and restaurant ablaze with lights, but the dock was mostly quiet, a variety of fishing boats and small yachts bobbing quietly in the water. A soft, cool breeze with a salty tang blew Alex's hair around her face, and crickets sawed night music in the grass.

It was so calm and peaceful. Alex had a hard time believing that anything sinister might be going on. *I guess we'll find out soon,* she thought.

They posted Louis as the first lookout at the VW.

Closer to the boats, they posted two more

lookouts while the last one went on to search the boat. Alex, who'd thought to bring a small flashlight, had volunteered for the job.

She went to the boat in the dark and stepped over the safety line alongside the deck—and gasped as the boat bobbed under her weight. She grabbed the line to steady herself and then made it onto the deck.

She listened for a moment to double-check that the boat was empty. Hearing nothing, she carefully went into the darkened deckhouse.

There was a small cabin light burning on the instrument panel in the wheelhouse compartment at the front of the deckhouse. Alex searched around with the small flashlight. She wasn't sure exactly what she was looking for, but she thought she'd know it when she saw it. She checked drawers and cabinets, and was just about to raise the lid on what looked like a foot-locker when she heard footsteps on the dock.

The boat bumped a fender against the dock.

She figured Henry or Megan must be following her onto the boat. She hoped the others were keeping a sharp lookout.

"Come over here," she whispered. "I need you to hold the flashlight."

But when she turned around the person she saw standing in the shadows wasn't Henry at all. And it wasn't Megan and it wasn't Nick, either!

It was a tall, bulky guy with a military crew cut and muscles out to here.

"Hey!" he cried. "Who—?"

Alex started to scream, but his thick hand went around her mouth and muffled the sound.

"No noise," the man grunted. Alex stiffened and his hand went away. She turned and saw the big man looming over her with a stern but slightly worried look on his face.

"No noise," he whispered again. Alex nodded.

Then he pulled her to the back of the boat, where she saw Henry sitting with a nervous look on his face.

"Sit down, kids," he ordered, pushing Alex to the deck next to Henry. He picked up Henry's camera and studied it like a bright, shiny toy.

"My boss will be back soon," he said to himself as much as to them.

"He'll know what to do with snoopy kids."

CHAPTER 8

Nick Stoll's charming smile had a threatening edge to it as he greeted Alex and Henry a short while later. "Well, hey, look what Mouse caught!"

"Mouse caught snoopy kids," the big man gurgled happily. Apparently that was his name, Mouse. "Snoopy kids," he said again, enjoying the approval from Nick. Then his expression changed to worry. "I think they looked in the trunk, Nick."

Nick frowned, especially when he saw Henry stuff his video camera behind his back. Then he let out a great big sigh. "My, my, my," he said with a sigh. "Didn't y'all's mamas ever teach you it wasn't nice to go snooping around in other people's things?"

"We know what you're up to!" Henry said bravely. "And we've got proof."

Alex groaned. *Brave, yes*, she thought. *But not particularly smart.*

Nick's blue eyes flashed with anger and his smile turned into a threatening growl. "I'm sorry to hear that, kid. Because I've got this little business deal going down, and I can't let anything— or anybody—get in the way." Nick thought a moment, weighing his options. "Tie 'em up for now. We've got an appointment to make." He waited till Mouse had tied them both up, then headed up the steps. "I'm sure you two will enjoy the ride out to the wreck site," he called back over his shoulder. "But I hope you brought your swimsuits. 'Cause it's a long swim back to shore!" Laughing, he climbed up onto the deck.

Another helper came aboard, too. "Hey, Mouse," the new man greeted the one who'd tied up Alex and Henry. "Nick says to loosen up the gags when we clear the marina—let 'em breathe a little. But you gotta put blindfolds on 'em then, so they won't know where we are."

"You kids better be good," Mouse said as he

tied towels over their eyes. "Or me and Jimbo here will make you walk the plank!"

Jimbo laughed. "Yeah, that's what Blackbeard woulda done!"

Hmm, Alex thought as the two men left her and Henry alone, *you guys just gave me an idea. . . .*

The ride in the back of the boat was bumpy and terrifying. The men had removed the gags, but they were blindfolded now, and not being able to see was worse than not being able to talk.

"Alex," Henry whispered, "are you all right?"

"Yeah, I'm fine," she whispered back.

"I'm sorry I messed up so bad."

"Henry—what do you mean?"

"I don't know," he replied. "I was so eager to get something on video, I walked right into their hands. I should've sneaked up on them and saved you. I have no idea what happened to Ray and Louis and Megan."

Alex grinned. "That's okay, Henry. It's not your fault. And I bet the others are going for help right now."

"You think so?" he asked.

"Sure. Can you see anything out of your blind-fold?" she asked him.

"Nothing!" he replied. "It's terrible. If I could just get one of my hands loose . . ." He struggled with the ropes, but the knots wouldn't budge.

"Don't worry," Alex told him, now that she was sure he couldn't see her. "I think I may be able to slip out," she grunted. "And I have a plan, too . . ."

A plan that doesn't include you. Not for now, anyway. He'd have to stay tied up. And definitely blindfolded. Alex couldn't let him—or the men in the cabin—see what she was about to do next.

"Stay here," she said to Henry. "I'll be right back." Quickly Alex turned her mind to things liquid—which was not difficult since she was on a swaying boat heading out into the ocean. Concentrating hard, she willed herself to morph into a puddle, which enabled her to simply spill out of her bonds.

"Alex!" Henry whispered. "Untie me! What are you doing?"

"Don't worry, Henry."

Henry squirmed against his ropes, trying to

111

get loose and follow her. "Be careful, Alex!" he whispered loudly.

Quickly Alex slithered up the stairs and flowed under the hatch to the deck.

A full moon shone like a spotlight on the dark rolling ocean, and she could easily see Mouse and Jimbo leaning over the side of the boat reaching down to Nick. He was wearing a black wet suit, which covered his entire head and body, and he carried an air tank on his back. Obviously he'd been diving. Were they at the shipwreck site?

Then she looked around.

Alex estimated that they'd been anchored in open water for at least a half-hour. She knew the men must be diving. Then Alex spotted Henry's video camera lying on a trunk just inside the deckhouse.

Rippling as quietly as she could, Alex oozed her way over behind a huge trunk lying just under the deckhouse roof.

Then, by concentrating, she silently morphed back into human form, crouching in the dark shadows behind the trunk. Silently she snaked her hand up to the top of the trunk and retrieved the video camera.

So far, so good.

There was some sort of thick-roped fishing net hanging off the side of the trunk, as though it had been carelessly tossed aside. The part of the net dangling down the side provided her with a sort of screen at the same time she managed to position the lens of the video camera through a hole in the net.

She knew the small bright lantern and flashlights the men were using would keep their pupils constricted and make it harder for them to see anything in the shadows clearly.

Yes, Dad, Alex thought, *believe it or not, I actually do pay attention in science class sometimes!*

Then Alex began to tape Nick and his goons at work. She wasn't sure how well the video would turn out, given the lighting, but she hoped she would be able to capture enough to make a case against the men.

Nick dived a couple of times while she watched, and each time he returned with a small object that she couldn't quite see.

I sure hope he's not diving for shells tonight! she thought.

Using the camera's zoom feature, she closed in on the object in Nick's hand. It looked like a thick, shiny metal disk—a coin. An *old* coin.

Alex grinned. As soon as they got out of this, she'd have some pretty hard evidence to show the police.

Assuming they got out of it.

When Alex felt her left foot falling asleep, she shifted slightly to get more comfortable.

Clang!

Something metallic fell off the trunk and struck the wooden deck.

Nick and his men whirled around, searching the darkness for the source of the unexpected sound.

Whoops! Alex thought nervously. *Time to put Plan B into action! And fast!*

Using her powers of telekinesis, Alex concentrated hard on the objects lying on the rough blanket on the deck.

She grinned as a brass bell rose in the air and flew past Mouse.

"Uh, Nick—" he choked out.

"What is it, Mouse?"

"D-d-did you see that?"

"What?"

"Th-th-th——" Mouse shook his head and rubbed his thick, meaty hand over his eyes. "N-n-nothing, Nick."

Alex waited a dramatic moment.

Then she slowly lifted a shiny coin from their stolen property and floated it next to Jimbo's ear.

Jimbo gasped, staring in disbelief, then frantically grabbed at the object in the air.

Alex flew it out of his reach.

"Aaaaghhhh! Nick!" he cried out.

"What!"

"Th-th-the stuff!" Jimbo croaked out. "It's . . ."

"Yeah . . . ?" Nick glared angrily at the man.

"N-n-never mind."

Nick shook his head. "Would y'all quit fooling around? We got a lot of stuff to do tonight. And I told you doofuses, this might be our last shot at this stuff. We gotta hurry."

"Sure thing, Nick," Mouse muttered.

Alex smothered a giggle as she saw Mouse force himself to stare at Nick and the lantern.

"And one of you guys go check on those

kids," Nick ordered gruffly. "Make sure they're still tied up tight."

Uh-oh, Alex thought. *Can't let anyone go downstairs and find me missing!*

Just as Mouse set the lantern down and headed toward the stairs, Alex quickly focused on a handful of objects and sent them all whirling around the deck.

Mouse shrieked and fell backward on his rear end.

Jimbo turned around to see what was wrong, and screamed.

It appeared as if the deck were alive with the floating treasures of the shipwreck.

Nick stared in disbelief. "What the—?"

"It's the curse!" Mouse shrieked, frozen in fear where he sat on the deck. "Blackbeard's curse!"

"My granny warned me against messing with shipwrecks!" Jimbo wailed, falling to his knees. "She said it was like stirring the bones of a watery grave—and she was right! Now we done it!"

Nick was apparently a doubting man, for he pulled himself onto the deck and strode toward the floating objects, grabbing at them, plucking them from the air.

"There's gotta be some explanation," he muttered.

"Yeah?" Mouse whined. "Like *what?*"

"I don't know!" Nick shouted. "Some kind of high pressure system—or wind—or magnetic field or something—"

"It's like the Ghostly Tramping Ground," Mouse moaned. "It's one of them psychic-type phenomena caused by the spirits of the dead walking the earth. And nothing you say, Nick Stoll, can explain it away!"

Just then Alex spotted something on the deck, something that could be the crowning touch to her dramatic display.

Lying amid the pile of supplies Nick had been using that afternoon to fix up the ship were a paintbrush and a can of dark red—*bloodred!*—paint.

Straining, Alex concentrated and removed the lid from the can. Her powers of levitating objects were not too precise, but she was able to float the can toward Nick—and dump the entire can of bloodred paint on his head.

This time all three men fell speechless at what appeared to be a dire warning from the ghost of Blackbeard himself.

Mouse fainted.

Jimbo hid beneath a tarp.

Trembling, never once looking back, Nick raced to the boat's wheel and turned over the engine, then floored it toward shore.

Startled by the boat's sudden jerk forward, Alex fell onto her side. But the men were too preoccupied to notice.

She grabbed Henry's video camera, then quickly morphed back into her liquid form and slid down the stairs.

"Wh-who's there?" Henry called out, still blindfolded.

As quickly and as silently as possible, Alex morphed back to normal, hoping she didn't gurgle too much in the process.

"It's me, Henry," she told him, hurrying to his side to remove his blindfold.

"Alex," he whispered, "are you all right?"

"I'm fine," she said as she struggled to untie the ropes that bound his hands and feet. Then she explained what was going on—sort of.

"Something's spooked them" is how she put it. "Mouse got it into his head that the site's protected by the curse of Blackbeard—"

"What!"

"Yeah"—Alex giggled—"and they even thought they saw the ghost of Blackbeard on deck warning them away!"

Henry rubbed his wrists where the ropes had chafed and stood up shakily. "I can't believe it. Those tough guys?"

"Well, you know, a lot of people are pretty superstitious about stuff like that," Alex said with a grin.

Henry looked at the stairs, a frown on his face. "So now what? Should I go up there and try to—"

"Nah," Alex interrupted. "I don't think they even remember we're down here. Let's just lock the door. I have a feeling that when we reach the marina, these guys are going to hit the dock running." She handed Henry his video camera.

"Oh, wow, I'm glad you found that. I think I may have gotten a few suspicious shots of them aboard the ship. I'm not sure if it'll be enough."

"Don't worry," Alex said, then decided to

keep it to herself that she'd done some videotaping herself. That way Henry would get the credit for the tape. "When I found your video camera, it was running."

"Really?"

"Yeah." Alex shrugged. "Mouse must have turned it on without realizing when he put it down. So it might even have some shots of their illegal diving activities. Enough to put them under suspicion at least."

"Super!" Henry said. "This'll be even better than the ghost of Virginia Dare!"

Here it comes, Alex thought.

"Uh, how's that project going, by the way," Alex said meekly. She was hoping he'd forgotten about that.

"Well, the news people won't touch it," Henry admitted. "But apparently somebody did pass my name on to a company that does special effects—for horror movies. They even called to offer me a job—but that's not really my thing. Horror movies, I mean."

For a minute there, you sure had me scared, Alex thought.

CHAPTER 9

THUNK!

Alex grabbed hold of Henry as the boat roughly banged into the dock.

The two teenagers looked at each other nervously. Would Nick and his thugs try to come down and drag them away to some hideout?

Then they heard footsteps on the deck above.

And then someone trying the doorknob. Then pounding on the door. "Open up!" someone shouted.

Uh-oh, Alex thought as fear trickled down her spine.

It was a man's voice—a voice they didn't recognize.

What should I do? Alex thought worriedly. *I could morph and escape, but that would leave Henry here alone. Or I could morph and take Henry with me. But then he'd know my secret. How—*

The knocking grew louder.

Alex made her decision.

She couldn't worry about what Henry might think of her GC-161 powers. The important thing was to protect him. Explanations she could think up later.

"Henry," she whispered, trying to prepare him for the weird experience that was about to happen to him. She laid her hands on his shoulders, preparing to morph and take him along with her. "Don't be frightened, but—"

"Kids! Are you in there?" a different voice shouted.

Alex and Henry stared at each other.

It was Stephen Driscoll!

Relief washed over Alex as another voice joined his.

"Henry! Alex! Are you okay?"

Henry finally found his voice. "Megan!" he shouted up the stairs. "We're here! We're okay."

Then he and Alex hurried up the steps, unlocked the door, and spilled out into the arms of

Stephen and Megan. The other man with them—
the first voice they'd heard—was a sheriff.

After they assured the Driscolls that they were
unharmed, Alex led them over to where the objects from the shipwreck had so recently been
flying around.

Sure enough, they were still there—only now
scattered innocently around the deck.

"Where are Nick and the other guys?" Alex
asked.

The officer pointed toward the main walkway
of the dock.

The handcuffed Nick, Mouse, and Jimbo were
being stuffed into a police car.

Nearby, Ray and Louis waved to them.

"When we saw Nick come back, I started to
come on the boat to make up some excuse about
how we were trying to sneak a party on Dad's
boat," Megan explained.

Stephen raised an eyebrow. "Oh, really?"

"Not that we ever would have," Megan hurried to add, "but I thought it would sound like
a good explanation as to why Alex and Henry
were on the boat and the rest of us were hanging
around the dock. But then Nick took off before

I could try out my story. So we called the police and then Dad."

"The Coast Guard has been out looking for you, too," Stephen told them, then shook his head. "I can't understand why Nick and his guys came back and ran off the boat."

"They were mumbling something about the curse of Blackbeard," the officer said. Then he glanced at the teenagers. "Do you have any idea what they're talking about?"

Alex shrugged. "I'm not sure. It was pretty spooky out there at night. Maybe they just got the jitters."

"Yeah, lucky for us," Henry said.

"I'll need you all to come down to the station and make a statement," the officer said.

"Sure, Officer," Stephen replied. Then he laid a hand on both Alex's and Henry's shoulders, his eyes filled with concern. "Are you guys sure you're okay?"

"Really," Alex assured them. "We're fine."

"They just scared us half to death," Henry joked.

Megan slipped an arm through his.

Stephen smiled. "Good. Now that I know you're okay, I can give all you kids my lecture."

"Huh?" Henry said.

"Um-hmm. About how stupid it was for you all to come out here alone! I can't believe you guys were so foolish. And Megan! What were you thinking, bringing your friends out here at night without telling us—"

Alex just grinned as she and Henry were led off the ship and onto the dock. She didn't mind Mr. Driscoll hollering at them. In fact, it felt pretty good.

She knew from her own parents that when they started giving you a hard time, it was a pretty good sign the danger was over.

Ray nearly knocked her down giving her a big hug. "Alex," he gasped, "are you all right?"

"You guys scared us!" Louis exclaimed.

"I'm fine," she said, then realized she was feeling a little shaky, now that it was all over.

Ray shook his head. "Louis, when you promised us this trip wouldn't be boring, you weren't kidding!"

Alex laughed. It was easy to laugh, now—now that she was back, safe and sound, with her friends.

CHAPTER 10

When the kids told the police the whole story of what Nick had been up to, Stephen Driscoll was amazed.

"Why didn't you kids just come to me?" he asked.

"We weren't sure about Nick, Uncle Stephen," Louis said. "We didn't want to come to you about an employee of yours without some kind of proof."

"I couldn't stand you being so miserable, Dad," Megan added. "I had to do something." Then she squeezed Alex's hand. "It was Alex's idea. If she hadn't overheard Nick in the gardens that morning, we would never have caught on."

Stephen shook his head sadly. "I'm disap-

pointed to find out it was Nick. I trusted him—
I trusted my whole business with him. I guess
I'm not a very good judge of character."

"How could you know, Dad?" Megan said,
slipping her arm around her dad. "He seemed
like such a likable guy. He had us all pretty
well fooled."

When the law enforcement officials played
Henry's tape on a small TV they had in the office, everyone was amazed at the shots they'd
gotten of Nick and his crew bringing shipwreck
artifacts to the surface and loading them on the
boat.

"This will go a long way toward making a
case against the men," the sheriff said. "And if
we're lucky, we can use Nick to get our hands
on the mysterious Mr. K."

"I can't believe what good footage you got,"
another officer said to Henry. "You said this part
was just an accident?"

Henry nodded. "I wish I could take credit for
it, but I can't."

"If it weren't for you carrying your video camera around," Alex put in, "we wouldn't have
any of this."

"That's right," Stephen said. "Henry, that's one piece of equipment you should never leave home without."

"Don't worry," Henry replied, obviously proud of himself. "First the ghost of Virginia Dare, now crime footage of shipwreck thieves. Maybe I ought to do this for a living."

Ray shot Alex a nervous look at the mention of Virginia Dare. But Alex just grinned and whispered, "Don't worry. I'll explain later."

Laura and Mr. and Mrs. Crompton had joined them at the police station, and when Stephen suggested they should all go home and get to bed, all the kids groaned.

"We're too wound up to sleep," Megan protested.

Laura put her arm around her daughter and led her to the car. "I don't know about the rest of you, but I could use a cup of coffee. How about a midnight breakfast at the pancake house?" she suggested.

The cheers were unanimous.

The next day Alex woke up with the mid-morning sun shining across her pillow.

Looks like the Driscolls let us sleep in, she thought.

Grinning, she sat up and threw a pillow at Megan. "Rise and shine!" she shouted, laughing as Megan sat up with her tangled hair in her face. "We've got four whole days left of our vacation—and I don't intend to waste a single minute!"

Soon they were dressed and banging on the guys' door.

Once they'd eaten their way through a box of cereal, they headed to the dive shop to see what was going on.

Stephen Driscoll was just putting a HELP WANTED sign in the window when the kids arrived.

"Hey, Louis, Ray—either of you guys interested?" he joked, nodding at the sign.

"No way!" Ray exclaimed. "Diving is way too dangerous for my tastes. Lifeguarding is more my style."

"I'll pass, Uncle Stephen," Louis said, flipping through some maps. "I think there's more money in artifacts. So tell me," he added, "how do you get a legitimate license to hunt for sunken treasure? Hey, have you ever tried using a metal detector on the beach?"

Stephen Driscoll just rolled his eyes at his nephew. "How about you, Alex?"

"It might be fun," Alex said. "Only—what's the shark situation on the Outer Banks?"

Stephen Driscoll laughed. "I wouldn't worry about that. I think it's the two-legged variety of predator that we've got to worry about the most around here." He pointed to his window. "Did you notice what good news I got this morning while you sleepyheads were still in bed?"

"Dad!" Megan cried, reading the notice. "The ban's been lifted! You're back in business!"

"That's terrific, Uncle Stephen!" Louis said.

"And it's all thanks to you guys," Stephen said, heading back inside to open his reservations book. "So listen, I've got to get to work here calling up some of these customers whose dive trips were canceled. But you guys be sure to be home by five or so. Laura and I are taking you all out to dinner—at the best place on the beach!"

"All right!" Ray and Alex slapped each other a high five.

*   *   *

"So how are we supposed to dress for the best restaurant on the beach?" Alex asked Megan. It was almost time for supper and they were waiting at the house for Laura and Stephen to get back. Alex dug through the drawer where she'd stored her clothes for the week. Should she wear shorts and the yellow shirt? Or should she see if Megan had a dress she could borrow?

"I don't know, it's weird," Megan said. "Louis said my dad just called and said *come as you are.*"

"We're wearing swimsuits!" Alex said.

"Louis said he told him that," Megan said.

Louis's voice came from the hallway. "They're here!"

Alex and Megan ran outside, followed by the three boys.

Stephen and Laura waved, then went around to the back of their pickup. Together they lifted out a huge metal tub and laid it on the ground.

"What's that?" Louis asked.

"Dinner!" Stephen said with a grin. "Come on, help out!"

The kids ran down the steps to the truck and helped unload. Firewood. Burlap tarps. A shovel. A metal bucket filled with clams on ice. A cooler filled with soft drinks and loaves of bread. Together they carried it all across the road, along the boardwalk, and down onto the beach.

The best restaurant on the beach was really *on* the beach. The Driscolls were treating them to a clambake!

They spread out a blanket, then Stephen showed the kids how to build a firepit below the high tide marker and use wet burlap to roast the clams slowly over the coals.

"This is so cool," Ray said as they waited to eat. "Do you think we could do this back home in Paradise Valley?"

Alex shook her head. "I guess we could do it in a backyard grill or something. But it wouldn't be the same."

"Yeah, I guess you're right, Al." Ray tossed a seashell at Louis. "We owe you, Driscoll."

"You bet you do," Louis replied, then frowned. "Uh, but for what, specifically?"

"For inviting us here, to the Outer Banks," Ray said.

"It's definitely the most un-boring place I've ever been," Alex agreed. "I'll never, *ever* forget it."

"Hey, who says you can't come back?" Megan

reminded them. "After all, the beach will always be here. And, hey," she added, smiling at Alex, "it's the absolute best place in the world for finding a summer job. All the shops out here are always begging for help. Maybe you could come back next summer! I know I could help you find something good."

Come back? Alex thought. *Next summer—for the whole summer?* The idea *definitely* had possibilities. She'd never been away from home for that long. But she might like it—especially with good friends like Megan and Henry.

Ray and Louis got a game of Frisbee going, and they all laughed at the "secret moves" Stephen shared with them from his college days, when, he claimed, he was a Frisbee champion. And there they stayed, and ate, and sang, and told stories until long after the sun went down and the sky burst with stars and the full moon rose and lit the beach like a stage.

About the Authors

CATHY EAST DUBOWSKI AND MARK DU-BOWSKI had a great time sending Alex Mack to one of their favorite places—the Outer Banks of North Carolina. They've been visiting the string of barrier islands since they were teenagers, got engaged on the island of Ocracoke, and later spent a year at Kill Devil Hill. No matter where they stray, they can't seem to shake the sand from their shoes and always find their way back to catch one more wave.

The Dubowskis have written many books together, including *The Mystery Files of Shelby Woo: Comic Book Criminal.* Cathy has also written the *Alex Mack* books *Cleanup Catastrophe!*, *Take a Hike!*, *Bonjour, Alex!*, and *Truth Trap!* One of the Dubowskis' books for younger readers, *Cave Boy*, which Mark also illustrated, was named an International Reading Association Children's Choice.

Mark and Cathy write together in North Carolina, where they live with their daughters Lauren and Megan and their golden retriever, Macdougal.

My favorite part of summer is

☐ anytime I'm not in the car.

☐ burying my dad in the sand while he's taking a nap.

☐ asking my mom "Are we having fun yet?" every five minutes and then telling her I was just reading the title of this cool activity book out loud.

Are We Having Fun Yet?

Summer Activities Inspired By

NICKELODEON MAGAZINE

 A MINSTREL BOOK

Published by Pocket Books

To find out more about NICKELODEON MAGAZINE, visit Nickelodeon Online on America Online (keyword: NICK) or on the Web at nick.com

1480-01

Read Books. Earn Points. Get Stuff!

NICKELODEON® and MINSTREL® BOOKS

Now, when you buy any book with the special Minstrel® Books/Nickelodeon "Read Books, Earn Points, Get Stuff!" offer, you will earn points redeemable toward great stuff from Nickelodeon!

Each book includes a coupon in the back that's worth points. Simply complete the necessary number of coupons for the merchandise you want and mail them in. It's that easy!

Nickelodeon Magazine.	**4** points
Twisted Erasers	**4** points
Pea Brainer Pencil	**6** points
SlimeWriter Ball Point Pen	**8** points
Zzand	**10** points
Nick Embroidered Dog Hat	**30** points
Nickelodeon T-shirt	**30** points
Nick Splat Memo Board	**40** points

- Each book is worth points (see individual book for point value)
- Minimum **40** points to redeem for merchandise
- Choose anything from the list above to total at least **40** points. Collect as many points as you like, get as much stuff as you like.

What? You want more?!?!
Then Start Over!!!

Minimum 40 points to redeem merchandise. See next page for complete details. Void where prohibited.
1464-01(1of2)

NICKELODEON/MINSTREL BOOKS POINTS PROGRAM

Official Rules

1. *HOW TO COLLECT POINTS*

Points may be collected by purchasing any book with the special Minstrel®/Nickelodeon "Read Books, Earn Points, Get Stuff!" offer. Only books that bear the burst "Read Books, Earn Points, Get Stuff!" are eligible for the program. Points can be redeemed for merchandise by completing the coupons (found in the back of the books) and mailing with a check or money order in the exact amount to cover postage and handling to Minstrel Books/Nickelodeon Points Program, P.O. Box 7777-G140, Mt. Prospect, IL 60056-7777. Each coupon is worth points. (See individual book for point value.) Copies of coupons are not valid. Simon & Schuster is not responsible for lost, late, illegible, incomplete, stolen, postage-due, or misdirected mail.

2. *40 POINT MINIMUM*

Each redemption request must contain a minimum of 40 points in order to redeem for merchandise.

3. *ELIGIBILITY*

Open to legal residents of the United States (excluding Puerto Rico) and Canada (excluding Quebec) only. Void where taxed, licensed, restricted, or prohibited by law. Redemption requests from groups, clubs, or organizations will not be honored.

4. *DELIVERY*

Allow 6-8 weeks for delivery of merchandise.

5. *MERCHANDISE*

All merchandise is subject to availability and may be replaced with an item of merchandise of equal or greater value at the sole discretion of Simon & Schuster.

6. *ORDER DEADLINE*

All redemption requests must be received by January 31, 1999, or while supplies last. Offer may not be combined with any other promotional offer from Simon & Schuster. Employees and the immediate family members of such employees of Simon & Schuster, its parent company, subsidiaries, divisions and related companies and their respective agencies and agents are ineligible to participate.

COMPLETE THE COUPON AND MAIL TO
NICKELODEON/MINSTREL POINTS PROGRAM
P.O. BOX 7777-G140
MT. PROSPECT, IL 60056-7777

NICKELODEON

MINSTREL® BOOKS

NAME_____

ADDRESS_____

CITY _____ STATE ـــــــ ZIP _____

THIS COUPON WORTH FIVE POINTS
Offer expires January 31, 1999

I have enclosed _____coupons and a check/money order (in U.S. currency only) made payable to "Nickelodeon/Minstrel Books Points Program" to cover postage and handling.

❏ 40–75 points (+ $3.50 postage and handling)

❏ 80 points or more (+ $5.50 postage and handling)

1464-01(2of2)